A

Norman George was born in Bangor, Co. Down, and grew up during the height of the Northern Ireland troubles. He attended Bangor Grammar School and then studied Biological Sciences at the University of Manchester. After a brief period of research on disease-carrying mosquitos, he switched to a career as an IT network specialist.

He maintained a strong interest in natural sciences while working in IT, reading widely, and completing an Open University degree in Geosciences. He spent over 20 years living and working in several European countries, including France, Belgium, Germany and Switzerland.

Having always been interested in Human Evolution and Anthropology, after a visit to Delos, he was inspired to write a novel about how the Greek gods might react to the current state of their ancient temples and over-tourism. *Divine Intervention* is the result. Hopefully, whoever reads it will find it both amusing and interesting.

Other work by Norman George:

Who Writes the Rules (…for living in an over-populated, multi-cultural, dying society). (Published 2022)

ISBN: 978-1-7392330-0-6

FIRST EDITION: November 2024

Cover Art: Norman George

Paperback ISBN: 978-1-7392330-2-0

Acknowledgements

Firstly, I must thank the male cats of Delos Island who, without the sacrifice of their manhood, this book would not have been conceived. In 2022, my daughter Louise was a member of a veterinary team that visited Delos to neuter the local tomcats that were decimating small mammals, lizards and birds on the island. As a consequence, I chose to visit the archaeological sites of Delos and Athens in 2023, a short trip which resulted in the conception of *Divine Intervention*.

Thank you to Mags for an important trilogy of functions:

- Accompanying me as my 'research assistant' on several trips to Greece.
- Having the patience to be bemused while my head was in conversation with various Greek gods.
- Proofreading and the initial editing of my first draft.

I am indebted to Julie Helliwell for her assistance and advice on formatting and the final editing necessary to turn the published novel into a professional-looking book. Julie can be contacted via her website, www.polishedpublications.com or by email at juliehelliwell@polishedpublications.com.

Table of Contents

Chapter 1: Athena at the Acropolis

Hector Johnson flinched and stepped back as he felt his bladder empty into his underpants.

"Damnit, Hector!" yelled his wife, Helen, as she spotted the wet stain on his crotch, spreading down his left leg. "I told ya, ya need to go see the doc about that prostate. Couldn't ya have held it in, or found a john?"

"It weren't me. She did it!" blurted out Hector as he turned back to look at Athena. But she'd vanished.

"Who did it? Who's 'She'?" asked Helen. "Have you flipped, Hector? You can't blame somebody else when you piss yourself!"

Hector scanned the crowds, searching for the strange lady. How did she do it? Who was she?

Behind a nearby column, Athena allowed herself a smug smile of satisfaction. You can't ogle an Olympian goddess and get away with it. He was lucky that it was Athena. Had he done that to Artemis, she would have turned him into a rabbit and dropped him in front of a fox!

Athena was livid. For 5000 years, the huge rock outcrop on which she stood had been the grand foundation stone of her temple. A spectacular platform that dominated the surrounding terrain, the rock was a gift of nature to the early settlers of Attica. Stone Age hunters and foragers had found a perfect haven where their encampments would evolve into homes and farms on the Attic Peninsula. Their chosen territory was rich, fertile and safe. Protected from aggressors by surrounding mountains and seas, their settlements grew into the city of Athens.

The metropolis had spread outwards around the vast natural fortress of the Acropolis rock—a massive, flat-topped limestone formation, from the base of which leaked several springs of pure water. Standing 50 metres above the surrounding terrain, the top of the rock was 300m long by 150m wide. It provided a fortress dominating the Attic plains and offered an almost impregnable citadel. From this stronghold, the Athenians had 360° views over the spreading city and down the 5km route to the huge natural harbour at Piraeus. The harbour provided a port and shelter for the trading and fighting ships that would come to control the routes to neighbouring islands and coastal communities.

Possession of the fortress and harbour had enabled the Athenians to progress over the centuries, becoming the most important sea-faring people on the lands surrounding the Mediterranean Sea. As Athens developed into a sea-trading city-state, it advanced the tenets of civilisation and shipped them to new locations around the coasts of the Mediterranean.

Throughout the march of history, Athena had watched over the city. She had observed as the temples that graced the Acropolis and the surrounding municipality had been built, fought over, destroyed, rebuilt, turned into mosques, churches or garrisons, then partly restored, or allowed to crumble to gravel. Across the millennia, the crowning glory had always been the Parthenon: the Temple of Athena. Erected at the zenith of her city, its stunning white limestone columns had stretched towards the sky, bearing an ornate temple roof embellished by intricate marble statues and carvings.

The early Athenians had worshipped the goddess Athena. She was the daughter of Zeus, the king of the Olympian gods. She symbolised Athens and the wisdom it exported. In the distant past, the people had offered sacrifices to her and held games and festivals in her honour.

Today, in the 21st century, Athena gazed at the ruined remains of the Parthenon. Only a quarter of the columns remained erect, and much of the remaining structure was covered by scaffolding and work platforms. The temple was open to the sky, the roof having been destroyed centuries earlier. Cranes and lifting equipment used for reconstruction stood idle in the middle of the floor.

The decorative marble statues and friezes had long since been removed, some being sent to national museums, others lost or destroyed. The floor and surrounding areas were half-covered by large limestone blocks and rubble pieces of varying sizes.

At the southwest end of the rock, hundreds of hot, sweaty people queued under the early summer sunshine. In recent years, mobs of cruise ship passengers disembarked at Piraeus to explore the city and its archaeological highlights. They now supplemented the already large number of Acropolis visitors, who formed long lines snaking to the ticket gates.

Once through the turnstiles, the visitors traipsed along a steep path and mounted an ancient, wide staircase leading to the congestion at the Propylaea columns. The Propylaea defined the entrance to the ancient fortress at the southwest end of the rock platform, forming the gateway from which visitors emerged onto the flatter terrain at the top of the rock.

A dense queue of people from many different nations around the planet wound like ant columns in slow-moving ranks. They tramped along designated trails enclosed by security fences to keep the crowds away from the archaeological restoration sites. Guards with whistles blasted out warnings to any tourist transgressing the protective fences.

Athena was conspicuous among the cosmopolitan mob that explored the ancient sites on the Acropolis. Her rich, golden-brown, wavy hair swept about her shoulders in the late spring breeze. Piercing blue-grey eyes shone from an elegant, intelligent face that exuded a regal beauty—not sexual but captivating and hypnotic, wise and dignified.

The smooth, golden-tanned skin of her body and face contrasted with a soft white fabric wrap-like dress. The garment hung from shoulder straps, flowing down and caressing the contours of her chest and abdomen. It was gathered tightly around her waist and held by a girdle decorated with gold-thread embroidery, exaggerating the smooth curves of her athletic torso. Brown leather sandals, secured by ties around her ankles, hugged her feet.

Few among the tourists paid any attention to Athena. To them, she was just another slightly eccentric-looking visitor to the rock.

Athena scowled at the crowds. They weren't here to pay homage to her. They weren't sacrificing lambs or goats, or celebrating her glorious matronage over the city. They weren't respecting her Parthenon. Some may have been a little in awe at the grandeur of its columns, or at least of those that remained in position. A few wondered how, 2500 years ago, people could have built such an impressive structure. How were the ancient Greeks able to design and construct those columns in such a perfect geometric arrangement that, if extended upwards, would have converged and met 13km above the surface of the rock?

Strolling among the mortals, Athena scrutinised the tourists with contempt. They didn't respect the crowning glory of the ancient city of Athens. They dropped little plastic bottles, food wrappers, cigarette ends, and chewing gum. They complained about the heat. They complained about the queues. They complained about the crowds. They complained about the security fences stopping them from entering the Parthenon and the other excavation sites.

They took lots of photographs, but so many selfies! Mostly ignorant of the Parthenon and its history, they were more interested in capturing their own grinning images with an ancient monument as a backdrop. They could WhatsApp it back to Tokyo or LA. Athena imagined many didn't even know what country they were in.

"Hi, Mom. I'm in Italy today!" Athena heard a young man say as he recorded a voice note. She rolled her eyes, seething inside.

Between Athena and the Parthenon, a slim, fashion model-shaped Japanese lady stood tall in platform shoes. Radiant in an electric blue dress of a shiny, silken fabric, she threw her head backwards and raised one arm towards the sky in a slow, waving motion. The other arm swept down and slightly backwards as she swivelled into different angled postures. Long, straight, black hair flowed around her shoulders while she writhed in a slow-motion dance before the front façade of the Parthenon. Her companion, an equally perfect specimen of Japanese youth, took multiple images of her gyrating friend.

"Don't I look great in front of this old ruin?"

At moments like this, Athena regretted the taboo associated with divine intervention. Not since the Trojan War, 3000 years earlier, had the gods interfered directly in the affairs of mortals. Zeus had decreed that they should desist after individually taking sides and influencing the outcome of the conflict. Even Odysseus's Trojan Horse idea had been devised by Athena herself: a ploy to ensure the Greeks won the war.

Athena did not feel guilty about her actions in Troy. She was the goddess of war, but her modus operandi was not that of a killer. She was a strategist who could shorten the conflict and thereby save lives. The wooden horse plan brought the

Trojan War to an end in its 10th year, after a long, stagnating campaign.

The gods had long agreed that they should avoid direct interaction with mortals. For some reason, it was better for people to "have faith" in the existence of deities. If the gods presented themselves openly to mortals, then there would be no need for faith. It wouldn't do for them to provide proof of their existence. They could watch in amusement while mortals evolved their own religious rituals and practices. The lives and deaths of people were predetermined by the Fates. Divine intervention was unnecessary and therefore banned by Zeus.

Athena had watched the two Japanese ladies take turns contorting into elegant poses among the limestone blocks and debris that were scattered across the terrain in front of the roped-off Parthenon columns.

People, young and old, had drifted past, pausing for selfies or group photos: a young boy on his father's shoulders, smiling at a mobile phone on an extendable stick; an elderly lady in a wheelchair, capturing herself, her middle-aged son behind the chair, and the Parthenon columns in the background, all on a personal device held at arm's length.

They would all stop, take their pictures, and then stroll on to the Altar of Zeus Polieus, protector of the city. This was the highest point of the Acropolis from which they could admire the view over the streets, bars, restaurants and ancient sites of the Monastiraki and Plaka districts. Orange roofs topped limestone and whitewashed buildings below. Streets teemed with people dipping in and out of souvenir shops, selling little models of Athena, Zeus, all the other members of the Olympian pantheon, and other useless souvenirs. Apartment buildings and office blocks stretched out from the old city commercial districts into the distance, where they seemed to melt into the olive-green colours of the hillsides beyond.

And then the Johnsons arrived—the straw that broke the camel's back.

"Hector, mind ya don't trip over that old rock!" Helen exclaimed with a Texan drawl. "Them darned sandals are far too big for ya. Ya can't walk in them without trippin' everywhere!"

Athena turned to scrutinise the origin of the voice. A pair of overweight, middle-aged American tourists, flushed from the effort of walking up through the Propylaea, trotted slowly towards her.

Cruise passengers, Athena rightly observed to herself.

Hector looked more like a displaced fisherman than an international traveller. A light-grey angler's gilet covered a long-sleeved, mustard-coloured, cotton polo shirt stretched across a distended abdomen. Beige cotton shorts covered his chubby thighs, protecting them from the Grecian sun. His feet were beginning to show signs of sunburn where they peered out of his open sandals. A beige bucket hat with a brown band kept the sun from a bald head. His greenish eyes were barely visible behind a pair of dark-rimmed, grey-lens sunglasses. A canvas satchel bag hung from his shoulder, containing some tourist essentials: water bottle, pastries salvaged from the breakfast buffet, camera, map of Athens…

Hector!? Athena was flabbergasted. *How dare they call him Hector?* she angrily thought to herself as she eyed this person who wasn't even fit to kiss the feet of the great Hector, Prince of Troy.

In the war, Athena had taken the side of the Greeks. She respected Hector for being the great warrior, honest and honourable man that he was. However, that didn't stop her from assisting Achilles to ensure he defeated and killed Hector in a man-to-man conflict. That was fate. It had been foretold. It had to happen. She was simply helping to end the war. It was exactly the sort of divine intervention that Zeus had since forbidden.

"I'm fine, Helen. Stop yer fussin'."

Helen!? HELEN!! Athena stopped in her tracks. "It gets worse," she mumbled with a sigh.

Helen of Troy had been the most beautiful mortal in the ancient world: a queen married to King Menelaus of Sparta. Aphrodite, the goddess of love, had promised Helen as a prize to Paris, Hector's younger brother, if he declared that she, Aphrodite, was more beautiful than her fellow goddesses, Hera and Athena. The subsequent abduction of Helen, who was taken under the protection of the Trojan Royal family, led to ten years of conflict and thousands of violent deaths.

Helen of Dallas, on the other hand, had never been described as beautiful, not even by her husband, Hector Johnston. He had always loved her more for her inner self than for any visual attractiveness. Now in her 60s, she was several sizes too large, with sweaty, greying hair and beady eyes. A flushed red nose and cheeks gave her a clown-like complexion beneath her dripping brow.

Helen's attire was intended to be practical rather than elegant, providing lightweight protection from the sun. A long-sleeved, blue and white floral-patterned linen top hung above a loose cream skirt that reached well below her knees. A wide-brimmed straw hat and sunglasses kept the sun at bay. Flat white canvas shoes were perfect for negotiating the tracks through the debris that blanketed the Acropolis.

Hector had caught sight of a rather beautiful lady who seemed to be examining him and his wife. There was something about her, like she'd stepped straight out of a cinema screen. She was obviously one of those strange European celebrities who appeared to glow without sweating under Mediterranean sunshine.

Finding it impossible to override his basic instincts, Hector scanned Athena's curvaceous form from top to bottom and back up again. However, on the way back up, his gaze locked onto the darker, bronzed line which defined the cleavage of her breasts. He hadn't intended to stare, but his eyes refused to move on upwards. Despite the camouflage of his sunglasses, Athena clearly saw exactly where Hector was looking.

I really do think we ought to reinstate divine intervention, thought Athena.

She had considered extending a virtual hand grip into his chest. With a firm squeeze, she could stop his heart. Nobody would know it was divine intervention. It would look like he'd had a heart attack, which would be blamed on the exertion of climbing up the Acropolis in Athenian heat.

Like all of the Olympian gods, Athena was vain and arrogant, but she represented justice and was rarely cruel. Hector's heart would not be stopped today. However, he was not going to get off scot-free. Athena extended the virtual hand, invisible to mortals, not to the heart, but a bit lower, to the base of his oversized belly.

Hector hadn't been aware of a fairly full bladder, but as he pulled his eyes away from Athena's cleavage, he felt a little pressure around his lower abdomen. His left thigh became warm, then cold, as his bladder contents leaked through his underwear and down his leg. He looked directly at Athena, who smiled as she returned the eye-to-eye contact before glancing down to view the darkening patch spreading across the front of his trousers.

Hector had turned back to Helen as she noticed the wet stain. Engrossed in admiring the ancient artefacts surrounding them, she hadn't seen Athena. Now she was stunned that Hector wanted to blame somebody else for pissing on his trousers!

Hector scanned the scene, but Athena was no longer anywhere to be seen. Did she go behind one of the Parthenon columns? But why didn't the security men stop her? That's behind the barriers.

"Ah tell ya, Helen. There was a woman there. Somethin' strange about 'er. Like maybe a ghost or somethin'."

"Hector Johnston!" exclaimed Helen. "It's not just the dick doc you need. You gotta see the shrink, too. Ghost?! Whatever next? We gotta get off this damn rock and go find you some new pants. Ya ain't goin' back to the ship stinkin' of piss!"

Hector thought hard. If he insisted on blaming his mishap on the mystery woman, Helen would never accept it. She'd want him to get counselling.

"Ahhh… OK, Helen. Ah don't know how that happened. Maybe it's the heat? Maybe ah drank too much water? Maybe ah will get the prostate checked up when we get home."

"We'd best get down off of here and go searching for some new pants for you. We've got Mykonos tomorrow and that trip to Delos. More damn old ruins to stumble 'round. We can go down to the shops, then head back to the ship."

Athena peered out from behind one of the Parthenon columns as Hector and Helen made their way back towards the Propylaea. There were plenty of shops in the streets of Plaka below. Maybe Hector could get something a bit more stylish than his shabby chino shorts?

It was saddening that the great city of Athens had lost its former glory—the city that gave the world civilisation, democracy and ethics. Now, the magnificent temples were crumbling and being trodden to dust by an army of tourists.

What would the other Olympians think if they saw the state of the place? But maybe they already knew. Perhaps they had all seen similar issues in other parts of Greece and elsewhere.

An idea was forming in Athena's sharp brain. Nobody worshipped the Olympians anymore. They had been consigned to mythology and history. It was time to gather the gods together once more to reflect on their insignificance in the modern world. She would invite them all to Athens for an Olympian reunion. Was it time to reinstate divine intervention?

Chapter 2: The Eagles of Mount Olympus

Mount Olympus stood majestic, rising up to 2900 metres above the nearby Aegean Sea to the east. On the northwest slopes, a cirque that had been carved into the mountain by glacier ice more than ten thousand years ago was now a dark grey cauldron, trapping and absorbing the heat of the afternoon sun. Incoming westerly breezes were warmed and deflected upwards towards the horseshoe ridge that defined the top of the mountain. A stream of thermal currents flowed to the summit and poured over the top, creating perfect conditions for soaring and gliding.

A dark object ascended out of the cirque, climbing slowly skyward, riding the crest of an airwave. As the rising speck soared above the ridge, it wheeled to follow the curve of the horseshoe toward the north. Stretching to the horizon in the south and west, cottonwool cumulus clouds flecked a bright blue, late spring sky. Silhouetted against the clouds, the outline of the flying creature became more defined. Outstretched wings spanned roughly 2.5m, each terminating in a line of primary feathers, pointing like fingers to the surrounding heavens. Its tail feathers splayed out fan-like, assisting the wide-spread wings to soar and steer its body, using the thrust and lift of the thermals. Like Icarus, before the heat of the sun melted the wax that held the feathers together on his wings, the creature toyed with the air currents, manipulating them and using their energy to pirouette, roll and circle around the sky effortlessly.

The creature's sharp vision scanned the land below as it glided along the ridge, turning east towards the sea and swooping above the scree slopes. As it descended, the underlying terrain metamorphosed from grey-white rubble to patchy-green scrub and then to the deep, rich green of coniferous forest.

In the mountainous forest below, the old monastery of Saint Dionysios stood proud, largely reconstructed after the Germans tried to destroy it in 1943, supposedly for harbouring Greek resistance fighters.

The bird, a golden eagle, played on the air currents. It circled the monastery before descending along the craggy, forested slopes towards the town of Litochoro. Skirting the town, it glided away from the pine forests over copses of plane and cypress trees, above olive groves and vineyards towards the beaches lining the shoreline.

Zeus had taken on many forms over the millennia, but the golden eagle was his favourite. The pleasures of swirling in the wind, relaxing while the thermals lifted him and held him high: they made him feel like a god, which, of course, he was! Zeus was the king of the Olympian gods, the father of gods, muses, graces, heroes, and the founders of humanity. And, of course, husband of Hera, his queen.

Since Zeus had first ruled Olympus, he was notorious for one serious shortcoming. Sex. He couldn't resist it. He wanted to seduce any female and quite a few males, immortal or mortal, who came within his grasp. Of course, he loved his wife, Hera, mother of the Olympian gods Ares and Hephaestus. But that was emotional love for his wife and queen. Lust was an entirely different matter. That was instinctive desire, directed at everybody and anybody.

Zeus liked to sneak away from Hera's gaze whenever the opportunity presented itself. Usually, he was in one of his many animal disguises. He would roam the countryside, cruise the skies, forests and meadows, towns, bars and beaches, always on the lookout for a potential object for his urges. The eagle was a particularly good option. He could travel quickly over a long distance, scanning the land below with razor-sharp vision.

For Zeus, the long line of beaches to the east of Mount Olympus was a favourite hunting ground. Along the coastline near Litochoro were several small holiday villages and campsites. Tourists and travellers would seek secluded sections of beach where they could sunbathe scantily clad or even *au naturel*. One of his favourite pastimes was to glide slowly above the shoreline, scanning for heavenly bodies.

And today, he was in luck. Cruising along the coast near Kalyvia Varikou, he spotted three ladies topping up their all-over suntans. Concealed from others on the beach, but not from the sky, by a low, grassy sand dune, they stretched out on beach mats in a sheltered clearing to enjoy a picnic lunch, undisturbed while soaking up the sun.

Zeus alighted on a pine tree branch at the edge of the beach, about 20m from the sunbathers—close enough for his eagle eyes to drink in a beautiful vision.

Daphne, Chloe and Tara had been enjoying a late spring sunshine holiday during their school half-term. A group of young schoolteachers who had studied and qualified together, they had kept in touch and enjoyed occasional reunions in interesting places, such as quiet Greek resorts with nice tavernas and nearby secluded beaches.

As a biology teacher, Daphne was amazed to observe a golden eagle alight on a branch of a nearby tree.

"Girls, girls!" she exclaimed as quietly as she could. "Don't move or do anything sudden, but a golden eagle's just landed in that tree over there," she said, nodding towards the back fringe of the beach.

Chloe and Tara very slowly turned their heads to look at the tree.

"Wow, he's gorgeous," whispered Tara. "If he was a man, I'd have him."

The girls giggled.

"Can we get a picture?" said Chloe, reaching for her mobile phone. "He's too far away for a selfie."

"Maybe we can entice him closer? Throw him something meaty?" suggested Tara. "What food have you got in your bags?"

"No. You'll frighten him off if you start throwing things!" said Daphne. "At least let me get some photos first."

Daphne carefully took a digital SLR camera from her beach bag. It had a telephoto lens zooming to 300mm, which allowed her to get quite reasonable pictures of the eagle.

"This is amazing. He actually looks as if he's watching us!" she observed.

Once Daphne had taken more than a dozen zoom shots, Tara again suggested throwing food towards the bird.

"OK," said Daphne, "but I'll just put the camera into video mode. Then, at least I can get him as he flies away."

While Daphne changed her camera settings, Chloe and Tara assembled a collection of cold meats and cheese pieces that they had rescued from their hotel breakfast buffet in order to have a snack lunch. They moved slowly and methodically, avoiding sudden jerks that might frighten off their majestic visitor.

"Ready, Tara. Let's see how far you can throw a lump of cheese without disturbing him," said Daphne, pointing the camera at the eagle and starting the video recording.

Zeus gazed towards the three ladies as Tara slowly rose to her feet, braced for a methodical toss, and then gently lobbed something in his direction. The cheese flew above the sand, landing among pebbles about 5m short of the tree.

Goodness me! he thought. *They're making me an offering! And I thought mortals had stopped worshipping us!*

The ladies were relieved that the eagle hadn't taken to its wings.

"Well done, Tara. He hasn't flown away. Will he come forward to take it?" queried Chloe.

Zeus pondered his situation. Here was a great opportunity to mix with some attractive, mortal ladies, as naked as the day they were born but considerably more mature and well-developed. He couldn't simply transform into a human in front of them. That would be breaking his own rules on divine intervention. Maybe he could fly out of sight, then wander back in human form and strike up a conversation. Being naked, they may not take too kindly to an approaching stranger, but he could make himself appear like Brad Pitt as Achilles in the film Troy. That would surely make the ladies very interested in conversing and more.

Shaking himself in a brief flutter, he glided down onto the hard ground a few metres away from the tree. He spread his wings wide for balance as he took a large hop forward.

"He's going for it!" Chloe said excitedly. "Are you getting this, Daph?"

"Yes. Got it all!" replied Daphne, as the eagle looked at her, then dropped his head to pick up the cheese.

"He's eating it! And he keeps looking up at us. Look at that glint in his eye, almost as if he wants to come over and thank us. Give him some more, Tara!" demanded Chloe.

Tara bent forward to pick up some more cheese. Zeus's beak watered as he studied the swing of her breasts and the sleek form of her body as she poised to lob another offering to the king of the gods.

The cheese landed a little closer this time, just 10m away from the group of ladies.

"Keep very still, girls!" said Daphne. "I can't believe he's coming so close."

"Maybe he's tame," suggested Chloe. "Maybe he lives with the monks up at the monastery or something. Do you think he'll eat out of our hands?"

"Don't be daft, Chlo," said Tara. "He's a wild bird of prey. He's just not frightened of us because he can fly away. He knows we've got food, so he's hoping for some more. Who would have thought an eagle would be so keen on a bit of Kasseri?"

"A bit of what?" asked Chloe.

"Kasseri. It's Greek sheep's cheese. That's what I've given him."

But Zeus was after a bit of something else. The cheese was an excuse for him to approach the ladies and admire their forms at close range, but he was already planning the rest of the afternoon in the form of Achilles.

I'll just go and pick up that other offering; then I'll fly off out of sight, he thought. *After a minute or two, I'll drop back around the corner and ask if they saw the golden eagle. They'll be dead keen to tell me all about it and show me the video. And I know they won't be able to resist a very fit Brad Pitt in a pair of budgie smugglers.*

Zeus smiled inwardly as he took a hop-step forward toward the next piece of cheese. He glanced admiringly at the girls, then dropped his head to pick up the offering.

"Shhrrreeeeeeee," a second golden eagle blasted in his ear as she dropped out of the sky, talons extended, clawing at his back before knocking him over.

The ladies all jumped back in surprise.

"Wow! Did you see that?" yelled Chloe. "He's been attacked by another eagle!"

"Surely they're not fighting over a piece of sheep's cheese?" queried Tara.

"See it? I've got it all on video. And they're still at it!" Daphne exclaimed.

"Shhhrreeeee, shhrreeee, ssshhhrrrreeeeeeee!" screamed the attacker as Zeus tried to dislodge himself from her talons. He pulled free and spread his wings as he fought to take off from the beach, under attack from his irate wife, Hera, the goddess of marriage and queen of the Olympian gods.

The three ladies watched on in amazement as the eagle under attack managed to free himself. When he flew off in the direction of Mount Olympus, his attacker, rather than pursuing, flew directly at them, shrieking its shrill "Sshhrrreeeeee, sshhhrrreeeeee!" A large splat of bird dropping landed right in the middle of their picnic arrangement.

As the women dived to avoid the angry eagle, it stretched a talon and clutched Daphne's camera, carrying it away as it turned inland and began a pursuit of Zeus.

"Hey, my camera!" cried Daphne.

As the bird left the beach, it released the camera, which dropped a good 10m before landing in adjacent undergrowth. Daphne pulled on a pair of flip-flops and a beach wrap to cover her as she fought her way into the scrubby, beachside vegetation in search of her camera, which she quickly retrieved.

"Is it damaged, Daph?" asked Tara.

"No. It got caught in a bush, which cushioned the fall. In fact…not only is it not damaged, but the video is still recording," observed Daphne before pressing the stop button to terminate the recording.

"Well, what about that, ladies?" added Chloe. "They were just like an old married couple having a fight."

"Yeah, like she'd nipped into the pub and found him chatting up the girls," said Tara.

"Or found him on a nudie beach with three beautiful, naked ladies," laughed Daphne, setting the trio into fits of laughter.

Daphne fast-forwarded the video to the point when the eagle had begun to move towards the second piece of cheese. They watched the viewer together as the sequence played out. The approaching eagle stepped toward their offering, and then wham! An angry eagle dropped onto him, screaming, like a Stuka dive bomber, scratching at his back. It then flew at them and grabbed the camera. As the eagle flew off, the camera pointed back towards them, capturing their stunned expressions before it rapidly fell into the undergrowth.

"Nobody would ever have believed us," said Tara, "but it's all there on the video sequence."

"We can't show that to anyone, though. Can we?" added Chloe.

"Whyever not, Chlo?" Daphne asked.

"Cos we're all starkers!"

The girls all guffawed once more.

"I don't see why not, Chlo," added Tara. "You've got lovely tits. Thought you'd be proud to show them off."

More fits of laughter.

"Ladies, after that experience, I think we may be downing a few retsinas, ouzos and anything else on offer tonight," suggested Tara.

If only they'd known how close they'd come to an encounter with Achilles!

Zeus flapped slowly, ascending gradually along the tops of the trees. He alighted on the roof of the old monastery. Hera glided around the building, then braked gradually, touching down on the roof a few wingspans away from him. Turning towards him, she glared directly into his eyes and screamed, "Sssshhhhhrrrrreeeeeeeeeee!"

"Oh, for goodness' sake, Hera. Nothing happened. I was just enjoying a glide along the beach, and some girls offered me a bit of cheese."

"A bit of cheese. A bit of cheese! I know you, Zeus. You would not have been content with a bit of cheese. When are you going to learn that you can't play around with the mortals? Or with the immortals, for that matter! You're my husband. You should be loyal and faithful."

"My dearest, you know I'm not mortal. It was my fate to help populate the Earth. You know that human moral rules don't apply to us gods. After all, you're not just my wife. You're also my sister!"

"The Earth has been over-populated already. It doesn't need any more help from you."

"My love, I'm also burdened with immortal genitals, ever in need of emptying. Surely you can't deny me that relief."

"If you seek relief, then remember who your wife is. And if I'm not around, then just relieve yourself. Stop chasing mortals!"

"You were a little mean to them, Hera. Why is it that if you are angry with me, you always have to take it out on the objects of my desire?"

"They were very lucky. I felt like ripping their little eyes out."

"Eagles don't attack people on beaches. What you did was a bit out of order. Imagine if you'd injured them. It would have made news headlines. Maybe frightened off tourists. Bad enough having jellyfish and sharks without man-eating eagles attacking the beaches."

"If you loved me, you wouldn't be interested in chasing mortals!"

"I've always loved only you! Mortals don't really matter. It's only lust that makes me do it, my beautiful wife."

As Zeus was trying hard to defend his consistently inappropriate behaviour, a familiar call crept out from a nearby pine tree.

"Whoo-whoo, whoo-whoo!"

Hera rotated her sharp eyes towards the source of the call. "Oh no," she groaned. "That's a little owl. Little owls don't call like that in the early afternoon. That's Athena. What does she want with us?"

"Athena!" cried Zeus in delight. "My favourite daughter!"

"But neither my favourite nor my daughter," muttered Hera.

Like the vast majority of Zeus's offspring, Athena was not borne by Hera. Her mother, Metis, was a wise and clever Titaness. She had raised and taught Zeus during his childhood before he eventually seduced her on the day of his wedding to Hera.

The seduction had been a complex chase in which both parties took on several different forms: Zeus in pursuit and Metis his prey. Afterwards, Metis had turned herself into a fly, at which point Zeus became a lizard and swallowed her. However, Metis remained inside Zeus, while Athena developed into a fully formed goddess dressed in armour inside his skull, causing Zeus an almighty headache. Hephaestus had released Athena by splitting Zeus's head with a battleaxe.

Eventually, Hera came to accept Athena as a goddess of justice, wisdom and war, and Zeus became immensely proud of the daughter who climbed out of his head.

Metis remained inside Zeus's head, tempering his excesses with words of calm and wisdom. This enabled him to maintain the respect and authority required for him to remain the leader of the Olympian gods.

"Athena, my daughter!" cried Zeus. "Stop hiding in the trees. Come and join us."

As Zeus and Hera gazed towards the forest, a little owl glided silently out of the trees and alighted beside Zeus on the rooftop.

"Any watching twitchers will be amazed!" laughed Zeus. "Eagles flying, not with doves but with little owls!"

"We're not flying, we're perching," corrected Hera.

"Reminds me of an excellent song," added Zeus. "… and the eagle flies with the dove. If you can't be with the one you love, honey, love the one you're with!" Zeus sang, then laughed as heartily as he could in the guise of a golden eagle.

"That's it!" yelled Hera. "You're mocking me now. I'm off," she added in disgust as she spread her wings and leapt from the parapet into a glide before flapping majestically and turning upwards towards Olympus.

"Maybe I'm just a mocking bird," responded Zeus, guffawing at his own witty response. "There's a mocking bird, singing songs in the trees. There's a mocking bird singing songs just for you and me," he added, crooning another old 1970s song.

"Oh, Father. It's sad to see you two always bickering like this," said Athena. "Why can't you stop winding Hera up like that? You need counselling, I think."

"From my wise daughter?" laughed Zeus. "What would you advise? Must I give up all life's little pleasures?"

"Maybe you should try to restrict your little pleasures to when you're with your own wife?" suggested Athena.

Zeus knew he didn't have a good counterargument for Athena. It would be best if he kept his inappropriate activity until nobody was looking. Unfortunately, Hera always seemed to be able to catch him out.

"Let's change the subject, my darling daughter," said Zeus, attempting to escape the criticism. "What is it that has given us the pleasure of your company? Is there something you need from us?"

"Only your support, Father," responded Athena. "It may have slipped your attention while your eye has been distracted by the hunt for life's little pleasures. However, it appears that we are no longer worshipped as gods. No sacrifices. No festivals. No prayers to be answered. And all of this has happened gradually ever since you banned us from using divine intervention."

"You know why I did that, Athena. The Olympians were taking sides and getting involved in the Trojan War. If I hadn't put a stop to that, then the result would have been conflict among the Olympians, which could have destroyed us completely."

"But we have been destroyed, Father." Our temples are in ruins, and we're insignificant in the minds of mortals."

"Then what do you suggest we should do, my beautiful, wise daughter?"

Athena contemplated for a moment and then replied, "I think we should gather all of the Olympian gods and goddesses together where the greatest accumulation of our temples once stood—in the City of Athens. We can debate what has happened to us and then vote on whether divine intervention should be reintroduced. Maybe that's what we need to re-establish our importance?"

A tiny voice in the back of Zeus's head told him that he should take heed of Athena's suggestion. Was it Metis?

"Maybe you are wiser than your father, Athena," Zeus replied.

"If you would be minded to gather the Olympians together, then if nothing else, it would be good to catch up. We can have a little party together. It will be interesting to get a few alternative views on how we should save the world of men and gods."

Athena was pleased that Zeus had agreed to her suggestion of an Olympian summit in Athens.

"Now, my daughter," said Zeus. "Let us go join my lovely wife on Mount Olympus and see whether I can grovel enough to restore her favour before we plan that big party in Athens."

With that, Zeus threw himself off the roof, extended his wings to a full 2.5 metres, and turned upwards in the direction of Olympus.

Athena considered the difficulty of an 8-inch tall little owl attempting that flight—a climb of 2000 metres up the mountainside.

"Sod that," she muttered inwardly, then transformed herself into a golden eagle before following Zeus skywards.

Chapter 3: The God of Anger and Violence

Near the border between Belgorod and Kharkiv, a rural house that had until recently been the home of a Ukrainian family had been turned into a Russian command post. Within a cellar, the most bomb-proof part of the building, Lieutenant Leonid Sokolov stared closely at a screen. A few years ago, he had enjoyed playing computer games. From flight simulators to dogfights and warcraft games, he was a self-confident, quick-thinking ace. On conscription to participate in Putin's "Special Operation", he had immediately requested that he train as a drone operator.

Sokolov's screen displayed camera footage from a drone that skirted the Ukrainian battlefront, some 10 kilometres south of the command post. Sokolov steered the device via a wireless signal, searching for signs of Ukrainian artillery, vehicles or personnel. From his safe distance, he could zoom the camera into potential targets. On a positive identification, he would then direct the drone toward the identified position until it struck, with its 6kg, high-explosive payload, destroying the target.

The Russians, too, were under attack from Ukrainian drones, each side playing a cat-and-mouse game. Search and destroy the enemy, just like a computer game. Each side used jamming devices in an attempt to block the transmissions between control centres and drones. However, many flying bombs were successfully deployed. Men were killed, and military equipment was rendered defunct.

Closely examining the screen, Sokolov spotted what looked like an armoured transport vehicle, partially hidden at the edge of a copse of trees. Zooming the camera towards the vehicle, he could detect definite movements. Somebody had exited the armoured car, perhaps preparing to launch their own drone bomb. Without hesitation, he accelerated the Russian drone towards the vehicle. There was sufficient explosive in the payload to destroy it, killing anybody inside and in the surrounding area.

The camera relayed images of two figures, who momentarily froze and then dived for cover as they heard and then spotted the incoming bomb.

"Too late," said Sokolov to himself, smiling as the image of the frightened foot soldiers raced out of the screen towards him before disappearing into a grey, fuzzy cloud as the drone signal died in the explosion, along with the targeted Ukrainian victims.

The explosion had destroyed the vehicle, killing its three occupants. One of the men who dived for cover was also killed. However, had there been a second camera filming the scene, Sokolov might have witnessed the other figure stand up and shake his fist in the general direction of the Russian forces occupying Ukrainian territory south of the border. Spattered with mud and debris, but no wounds, no bleeding, no injuries.

The figure snarled, his eyes glaring in fury, his long dark hair flecked with the flesh of his companion, but himself unhurt by the explosion. Being immortal, Ares was physically unaffected by the explosion. However, he was angered by the attack and upset at the death of his comrades, whose bravery he had come to like and admire despite his normally unfriendly disposition.

The least endearing of the gods may have been a darling son to Hera and a passionate lover in Aphrodite's mind. However, to the rest of the gods, his father Zeus included, he was a mean bastard. Ares, the god of war, was best described as angry, aggressive, nasty and unforgiving. He symbolised the passion and hatred which pushed men to kill each other in fierce hand-to-hand combat. He was the force which could drive a man to plunge a sword, spear or dagger into an assailant. To twist the blade, ripping vital organs. To sever limbs before striking the blow that released a final breath.

Although Athena was the goddess of war, her methodology was strategy and planning: to strive for victory and minimise bloodshed. Ares had no strategy or planning, only menace. He was a god of violence.

Throughout the ages, Ares had attended battlefields, seeking to inflame and encourage the combatants until they were sufficiently enraged to fearlessly kill or be killed. Sometimes, he chose sides in battle, such as the Trojans against the Greeks, or the Ukrainians against the Russians. Since Zeus had barred divine intervention, he couldn't actively fight, but he could still attempt to coerce and motivate his comrades into battle.

For Ares, life had been like a busman's holiday for most of the period since the dawn of civilisation. He liked to blend in with the combatants in any battle, to stir up and encourage animosity and anger. He would jeer and cajole comrades, pushing them to perform unspeakable acts of cruelty and violence. Mutilating and killing, then glorying in reaping the spoils of war; theft, rape, murder and destruction.

Humanity needed no faith or belief in Ares to drive them into conflict. It had always been simple to polarise groups who'd clashed over religion, territory or control of resources. Ares had always been happy to flit from side to side, provoking hatred and aggression at every opportunity. The

Mycenaean Greeks versus the Trojans, the Roman conquests, the Huns, the Crusades, Protestants against Catholics, Israelis vs Palestinians... Human history was an endless series of opportunities for releasing pent-up anger as horrific, violent acts.

As human populations expanded, they exploited more and more territory, turning forests and meadows into farmland and settlements. The causes of conflict increased, and the power and lethality of weapons evolved until humanity was on the verge of self-destruction.

In the twentieth century, world wars and Cold War-driven proxy wars meant there was always some battle for Ares to influence. In the twenty-first century, the major political powers vied for economic control and superiority. For some regimes, it seemed that the reason for their existence was to perform sly manipulation with the aim of causing economic turmoil among their competitors.

Ares had been busily inflaming the mayhem in Eastern Ukraine. He had been enjoying himself immensely, but was well aware that the political madness behind the conflict would long continue to play out without his assistance.

However, the god of war was troubled by the latest technological trends in warfare. For millennia, he had relished his role in stirring up hatred, inspiring combatants to drive the cutting edges of their weapons to the most vulnerable positions on an adversary. But now, warfare was fought using drones, missiles and remote-control centres, which usually meant that combatants never came into face-to-face contact. Conflict was done by computers and electronic devices, not by angry men! Men like Sokolov could calmly kill from a safe distance—without any need for anger or direct violence.

Did the god of war still have a purpose? Did the god of war ever have a purpose? Did war ever serve a purpose?

Ares reflected on his own history. In the days before civilisation, he didn't exist. Hunter-gatherers did not have wars. Humans lived in small groups: extended families or small tribes without fixed settlements.

They followed the herds of animals that usually moved seasonally in search of grazing land and water. It was only if they came into competition with another such group that there might be a skirmish for the control of access to food. At worst, if this occurred, some people might receive serious or fatal injuries.

Wars didn't happen until people formed settlements. Once they discovered that they could corral livestock and plant seeds of food crops, they began to claim ownership of land. They built homesteads and villages, which consequently required protection from potential marauders. Villages increased in size to become towns or marketing hubs for neighbouring towns. Increases in local population size meant more manpower to call upon for the protection of the community. The first militias and armies were born.

The birth of armies made it possible to wage war. Whether due to economic competition, greed, malevolence, or a desire for power over neighbouring peoples, the leaders of armies ordered their warriors into conflicts that would determine the future and soon become history.

The winners of wars would write the history, or at least relate the stories to pass down to future generations. Invariably, it was the winners who claimed to have the god of war on their side. He drove the heroes to show their courage in defeating and killing the enemy. Subsequent generations would pray to and offer sacrifices to the god of war to ensure their victory in any future battles.

Ares had been created by civilisation. It was only when there were growing towns and cities to protect that people went to war with each other and, therefore, needed a war god to take their side. As civilisation became more advanced, the gods of the victors in each war became established as the ones who had listened to the prayers of the winning side.

By the time of the Trojan War, Ares was well established around the Aegean as the Olympian god of war. However, he had taken the side of the Trojans, the losers. As Athens strengthened its position among the city-states of the ancient Greek world, Athena came to dominate as the Greek goddess of war.

Athena masterminded the ploy of using the Trojan Horse to sneak through Troy's defence. She had shown that, in an effort to gain the upper hand, strategy can outwit brute strength and violence. At the height of Athenian leadership of Greek civilisation, Athena, the protector of the city, became the symbol of the power of Athens.

Since the Trojan War, Ares had become a diminished figure, almost a lesser god, manipulating in her shadow. People at war could still be angered into committing atrocities, but war was changing. Maybe he was becoming superfluous.

Ares found it a curious thing about battlefields that, away from the immediate vicinity of explosions, the birds were still happy to sing. Some species even became well-fed with the human equivalent of road-kill. Chunks of human flesh, often tenderised by the pressure from a blast, were liberally distributed for the crows and scavengers. First come, first served. Other species simply sang, advertising themselves to potential breeding partners, oblivious to the blood being spilt around their fields.

An unusual birdsong caught Ares' attention. Unusual in that it was in the wrong place at the wrong time of day. Something nostalgic switched his thoughts away from the drone and the sad loss of his comrades.

"I'd know that shrill little whoo-whoo, whoo-whoo, anywhere! Have you come to join in a new war, Sister?"

In an instant, a little owl that had been perched on one of the copse's surviving trees dropped onto the ground and transformed into a fully formed Greek goddess dressed in camouflage fatigues.

"I'm not sure I like you calling me sister, Ares," replied Athena. "We may share a father in Zeus, but so did half the demi-gods, heroes and early humans of ancient Greece."

"My, my, Athena," laughed Ares, "you look just the part. Are you going to take on Russian drones?"

"I see you weren't too effective against that last one, Ares."

"You know I couldn't have stopped it without divine intervention. Which, of course, is against our father's will. So, are you going to stop the war?"

"Maybe," Athena responded, reflecting that the upcoming discussion on divine intervention might have a useful application in Russia.

"What's your plan? A big wooden bear at the gates of Moscow? Who's going inside it? Zelensky? Or maybe just some Ukrainian conscripts. They're all brave men, but you don't have an Odysseus here in Ukraine."

"No, Ares. I came to talk to you, not to Putin. You're more likely to listen," said Athena with a smile.

"Really? You think us talking will end all this?"

"No, Ares, but maybe we can persuade Zeus to drop the ban on divine intervention. Our importance as gods has been allowed to decline to insignificance since the Trojan War."

Ares found Athena's comments intriguing. She was right. He had spent several thousand years trying to encourage conflict and enrage combatants but without any real power.

Would Zeus allow the Olympians to directly intervene once more? If he could have deflected a bullet at Waterloo or shifted the bomb in the briefcase at Hitler's Wolf's Lair, then history could have been changed in the direction of his choice.

"So, what's your proposition, Sister?"

Athena frowned.

"Well, Half-Brother, I am calling for a reunion of the Olympians in Athens three days from now. We can all see together how the greatest of the old temples and places where we were worshipped have been allowed to decline. They're now infested by tourists from all over the world, who have little respect for us Olympians."

"And what do you think we can do about that?"

"Well, at least we can all put pressure on Zeus to allow us to use our power to change modern opinions. To make people see what we represent and why they should worship us once more."

"I'm not sure all the Olympians will agree with you, Athena, but maybe it would be good to get together and talk about it. For me, it would make a change from watching my friends being killed," said Ares, with an air of sadness.

"You have friends?" Athena seemed surprised.

"I'm not as nasty as you think I am," Ares said with a faint smile.

"I'm not sure your brother Hephaestus would agree," said Athena, "particularly while you're screwing his wife!"

"That's a mean thing to say, Athena. You know Aphrodite and I were always meant for each other. Hephaestus tricked Zeus and Hera into him taking her as his wife."

"That's beside the point. Aphrodite and Hephaestus were married with the blessing of Zeus and Hera. You and Aphrodite should not be cheating."

"Hephaestus knew the score. For him, Aphrodite was a prize bride. She's out of his league, and he knows that. So, he turns a blind eye. He ignores me meeting with Aphrodite, just as long as there are no witnesses."

"That doesn't excuse you. It's a matter of principle. Aphrodite is breaking her sacred vows, sworn before all the gods."

Uncomfortable with the conversation topic, Ares attempted to change its focus. "Have you persuaded any of the other gods to join you in Athens?"

"I've only seen Zeus and Hera so far. Zeus has agreed, and Hera won't let Zeus out of her sight, so she'll be there too."

"Can't blame her for that," muttered Ares. "It seems that breaking fidelity vows is simply following our father's fine example as a leader!"

"Well, it's morally wrong, no matter who's doing it," asserted Athena.

"Maybe none of the others will join you if you keep questioning all our morals," said Ares.

"Unfortunately, most of them have questionable morals!" noted Athena. "I don't know whether they'll come along or not, but it's worth trying to persuade them."

"When you see Aphrodite, tell her I'll be there. Then she's bound to add her sweet voice to your discussion."

Athena eyed her half-brother suspiciously. "If you're only coming along to cavort with Aphrodite, then I'd rather you didn't join us."

"Of course, I'll be pleased to have her wonderful company again, but my motivation is more than that, Sister. I've been feeling a bit down lately."

"What's changed, Ares? You've been down since you came into existence!"

"Surely you haven't come all this way to insult me, Athena? I actually agree with you about our loss of status among mortals. It feels as if they don't need a war god any more. They don't make offerings to me or pray to me for victory. In the last century, they've elevated their own war gods, who act with impunity. Politicians, dictators or religious leaders: they're all the same. Between greed and social differences, they brainwash their followers into hating their supposed enemies, then order conflict."

"So, what's your role then, Ares?"

"I don't have one any more. I've been trying to fire up hatred between the Russians and the Ukrainians, but even if I succeed, it isn't actually necessary on the battlefield. The combatants never get close enough to see the eyes of their enemies. They're all killed from a distance. Bombs, missiles and bullets. They don't even need to be angry when they do it. In fact, if the fighters stay calm, they can take aim more systematically, with greater accuracy. The only close-quarter killing is when the Russians murder their captives. And even I don't agree with that."

"We didn't complain when Achilles murdered captive Trojans. What's the difference?" asked Athena.

"The rules have changed, Athena. Humanity has had three thousand years of civilisation since then."

"My, my, Ares! You're going soft in your old age," said Athena, laughing.

"You surprise me, Athena. You, who represent justice, must see that sort of behaviour is wrong?"

"You're right, Ares. I'm just a bit surprised to see that you might have a sentimental side. I thought you might be the most difficult to convince that we have a problem because there are always wars going on somewhere. So, I thought you would be happy."

"Then why come to me first?"

"Well, I thought if I could convince you to join the debate on divine intervention, then I can convince all the others. Besides, you were furthest away, and Mount Olympus was en route to Ukraine from Athens. I had to get Zeus to agree before talking to the rest of the gods. The others will be easy."

"You can count me in. What's your plan?"

"From here, I'm going to head to the Aegean via Cyprus, where I can join your pretty lover on the beach before going to see the others. The plan is to meet late afternoon in three days' time on Areopagus Hill. Then we can have a day or two in Athens to review the state of things and have our debate."

"This was an awful long way for a little owl to fly, and Cyprus isn't quite round the corner. Surely, you're not..."

"Certainly not. Divine powers are only forbidden when humans might witness them. My little owl will do a time-warp flight to Cyprus. I'll be there in a few minutes. Meanwhile, I'll have a little dreamtime conversation with Artemis and Hermes so they can help me gather the gang together."

"Well then, Sister. It seems you've got a plan all worked out, as usual. I'll see you in Athens in three days. Send my love to Aphrodite."

"I'm sure you're already sending her too much of it!" said Athena sarcastically.

"You can never have too much love, Sister," said Ares, smiling uncharacteristically.

"That, from the master of hatred! Whatever next?" queried Athena as she disappeared from the battlefield.

Chapter 4: The Twins from Delos

“Can’t you knock on the door like a mortal would? I might have been naked. You shouldn’t just flit in like that. Somebody might have seen you through the window!” Artemis complained.

“What’s the problem, Sister? Don’t worry; I’ve seen it all before. Anyway, nobody saw me arrive,” Apollo replied. “I got your telepathy. You’re the one that called me here, to your fancy suite.”

Artemis had been manipulating a silver crescent-moon-shaped hairclip to hold back a long, dark fringe from an otherwise short, tom-boy haircut when Apollo suddenly materialised on the sofa across the room. She flashed disdainful, piercing blue eyes at her twin brother’s reflection in her bedroom mirror.

Slim and athletic, she wore a short, camouflage-patterned cotton dress pulled in by a leather belt around her waist. Artemis reached to fasten the ties of her sandals around her ankles. She was the goddess of the moon, the mountains, the forests and wildlife, as well as the protector of women during childbirth. The huntress, the avowed virgin who would always remain chaste, she represented the freedom and youth of women before motherhood. The original feminist, Artemis could shoot a deadly-accurate, silver arrow at anybody who might attempt to defile her.

"We can't just flit around materialising anywhere, Apollo. You know the mortals panic if they see that. There'll be newspaper reports of UFPs!"

"UFPs?" Apollo looked puzzled.

"Unidentified flitting persons!"

"I'm not a person. I'm an unidentified effin' deity! A UFD!"

"Just don't do it," Artemis replied sternly. "We have to look like and behave like mortals while we're among them in Greece."

Apollo pouted his lips like a sulking teenager. Tall, blond, blue-eyed, beardless, with a smooth, hairless chest, Apollo was the archetypal model that Hollywood relied on for casting deities and heroes and for designing cartoon characters. Bronzed skin and rippling muscles covered a solid frame, which might have suggested his endowment was brawn, not brain.

However, Apollo was far from stupid. He had unmatched knowledge of medical matters—he was an expert in diseases and healing. He could foresee the future and was always truthful. Unfortunately, his predictions often produced more questions than answers.

Like his twin sister, Apollo was a skilled archer. A remarkable musician, dancer and singer, he was often the life and soul of a party.

"So why the summons to Mykonos?" he asked. "I was happily plucking my lyre in Delphi when your thought waves interfered with my harmonics!"

Artemis had checked into the boutique hotel overlooking the Old Port at Mykonos Town the previous evening, registering under the name Diana Hunter. That always seemed to raise less eyebrows than Artemis Olympian. She'd told the receptionist to expect her brother, Pol, who would be sharing her two-bedroom suite. Apollo would have to flit out again and check in properly at the reception desk.

The hotel was constructed on several terraces arranged up the sloping hillside. Half a dozen cuboidal, whitewashed buildings with pale blue painted doors and window frames were arranged on either side of natural stone-paved paths that weaved their way up the gradient. The paths, interlinked by short flights of steps and bordered by dazzling white walls, led to individual guest suites. Along the crazy-paving, occasional slabs were engraved with dolphins and other marine animal motifs.

"Athena wants to have an Olympian's nostalgia trip to Athens. She came to me in a dream," explained Artemis.

"Why can't she just make a phone call like the mortals do?" Apollo demanded.

"She's a goddess, not a mortal. Besides, she likes to get inside my head. She finds that more intimate."

"I had Aphrodite in my head most of last night, but that wasn't as intimate as I would have liked," Apollo remarked with a smirk.

Artemis frowned at her brother's inappropriate suggestion. "Leave Aphrodite alone. She's married to Hephaestus. He wouldn't be impressed!"

"Ugly little Hephaestus!" Apollo sneered. "With such a lovely lady! It's a shame when she could have me, the ultimate in beautiful godliness."

"And you're so modest too, Apollo! Leave the other gods alone. Why don't you stick to molesting some pretty mortals like our father would?"

"Ahhh! You think, as the bastard son of one of Zeus's extra-marital frolics, that I should have inherited some of his behaviour? Ten thousand years old, and he'd still screw anything that moves. I'm not quite that bad," Apollo responded to his sister's suggestion. "But maybe I can take you out to a club tonight, Artemis. You've been a virgin for millennia. It's time for the huntress to chase down some mortal prey."

"You know I don't do men, Apollo, mortal or immortal. I'll take you to a gay bar. Mykonos has a few of those. The boys will swoon when they see a sun-bronzed marble statue strolling into their midst," Artemis laughed.

"So, now that I'm here, what's the grand plan?"

"I thought we could take a trip out to Delos tomorrow to our old childhood stomping ground. Then, when Athena's ready, we can take a ferry to Piraeus to join the other Olympians for the big reunion."

"A ferry!?" Apollo replied in horror. "With Poseidon wrinkling the sea and rocking the boat! If we must behave like mortals, then why can't we fly?"

"Do you have a passport, Apollo?"

"A passport?" I'm a Greek god! Why would I need a passport?"

"You're an ancient Greek god, but if you tell that to the airport security people, I don't think they'll just wave you through to the departure gate!"

"Fine, we'll take the ferry. I'll just have to get used to the sea with a little trip to Delos tomorrow."

"Now, Brother," said Artemis. "I'm going to soak up some sunshine by the pool. That's what mortals usually do in a place like this. I suggest you flit off again and walk back in by the reception like you should have done the first time."

"Fine," replied Apollo. "Grab me a sunbed, and I'll see you shortly."

Before Artemis could reply, Apollo had disappeared. She quickly changed into a camouflage-patterned bikini and threw a bath towel over her shoulder. She stepped into flip-flops and out the door, turning the room key in the lock as she left.

Trotting down the steps, the huntress passed by the reception area in the main building, arriving at the pool in a courtyard below. Sitting in front of the hotel but above the access road below, the pool surroundings offered an uninterrupted view of the harbour.

The pool was large enough to cool down in on a hot day but a little small for actually swimming. An adjacent spa pool provided an additional amusement option, with room for up to six people among the water jets. The sound of a fountain that poured into the spa might have fooled a snoozing sun-bather into imagining they were in a clearing by a river.

"Not the kind of mountain stream music I usually listen to," noted Artemis as she arrived by the pool just in time to grab the last two sunbeds for herself and Apollo. None of the others were occupied, but they all had towels strewn over them, whose owners were either still having a late breakfast or had gone on morning excursions.

From her sunbed, Artemis had a panoramic view stretching from the New Port, nearly 2km away on the right, across the open bay below. To her left was the Mykonos Old Port, a traditional fishing harbour that pre-dated ferries and cruise ships.

The New Port incorporated the ferry terminal, from where boat services to other islands and to Piraeus would arrive and depart throughout the day. Alongside the New Port piers, there was sufficient space for a single cruise liner to dock, but there were often at least three cruise liners trying to visit Mykonos simultaneously. The later ships had to weigh anchor in the middle of the bay in order to permit passengers to visit the island.

The Old Port provided a pier for boats running excursions to the island of Delos and for water taxis ferrying cruise passengers between their ships and the centre of Mykonos waterfront.

Artemis lay on her sunbed, with her upper body raised by the tilted headrest so that she could read her book, "The Huntress" by Kate Quinn. Looking out across the bay, directly in front of her, she could see a twelve-deck, 250-metre-long cruise liner anchored less than 1km away. A second cruise ship was already occupying the available dock space in the New Port.

From the cruise ship in the bay, a loud but unintelligible message streamed out of a tannoy system. The muffled, nasal voice seemingly poured out instructions to passengers boarding frequent water taxis bound for the Old Port. The stench of boat fuel and exhaust fumes crept constantly from the sea onto the shoreline.

A flotilla of sea taxis, each with a capacity of several dozen passengers, shuttled back and forth with their payload, like ants using a well-defined trail to move food to their nest.

Artemis exhaled a disappointed sigh. She had spent a short time by the pool the previous evening, watching the sun sinking behind the island of Syros, 35km to the west. It had been quite serene then, as the cruise boats had left already left port to travel slowly overnight to their next destinations.

As she was watching the scene below, a few other hotel guests appeared around the pool. Some fumed at the pre-reserved sunbeds and at the lack of alternative space where a towel might be laid in the sunshine.

Two gentlemen were approaching her. One was an athletic, he-man type who obviously enjoyed working out in the gym. His companion was rather effeminate, with a mincing waddle. Justin, the athlete, and Bernard, the mincer, were very good friends; both too promiscuous to be monogamous partners. They had come to Mykonos hoping to enjoy a fun holiday, having heard that it had a reputation as a gay playground.

Bernard smiled at Artemis as he passed.

"Morning, darling," he sang as the two arrived at a pair of adjacent sunbeds covered in brightly coloured towels, one a patterned pink and purple, the other a full rainbow.

Artemis returned Bernard's smile. While she would not normally encourage the company of men, she knew she was not in any way threatened by Bernard and Justin.

"Good morning," she responded with a friendly tone.

Bernard and Justin removed their shirts to reveal budgie smugglers that just about hid their contents. Justin's seemed to cling well to his firm frame, while Bernard's were seriously overhung by a pot belly.

"It's a busy, bustling day below on the bay!" Bernard continued, almost singing.

"Yes, it was peaceful here yesterday evening," Artemis responded, "but since those ships arrived, it has become noisy and smelly."

"All part of the atmosphere," said Bernard. "The town will be lively and buzzing. Great place for people-watching on the waterfront."

Justin, who had remained quiet until now, felt inclined to disagree with his friend.

"The lady's correct, Bernard," he stated. "It's noisy and smelly. The shiploads don't add to the atmosphere; they pollute it. All those little boats going backwards and forwards, pumping out fumes! It'll be like D-Day through the morning and Dunkirk when they all have to get back late afternoon."

Bernard frowned. "Don't you think the crowds add to the buzz? To the excitement of the island?"

"No, Bernard. There are too many people. And they're not the exotic, beautiful people who go to the bars and clubs or decorate the streets in the evening. They're shoddy crowds, wandering aimlessly through shops selling overpriced junk. They make the bars and restaurants too busy and the service too slow. The quality is dropping, too, because the staff are rushing around trying to handle large numbers of customers. The prices go up, and the quality goes down."

Artemis grinned in amusement. Justin was obviously the more sensible of the two men.

As they spoke, Apollo strode confidently from the hotel building towards Artemis, looking every bit like a Greek god. His open shirt revealed strongly defined abdominal and pectoral muscles, between which a golden laurel wreath pendant swung rhythmically as he walked.

"Oh my!" exclaimed Bernard as Apollo stopped at the sunbed next to Artemis. "I think I've died and gone to heaven!" he continued. "Is this your boyfriend? Or husband maybe?" he blurted to Artemis.

Before she could answer, he decided it was time for an introduction.

"I'm Bernard," he told the twins. "And this is my good friend, Justin," he added, waving a hand towards his partner.

Artemis smiled bemusedly at Bernard, who was obviously excited by the appearance of Apollo.

"I'm Diana," she said, "and this is my brother, Pol." She glanced briefly at Apollo.

Apollo glanced back at Artemis disdainfully. He disliked the deception of disguising their names. It was bad enough pretending to be mortal.

"Paul?" queried Bernard, extending his hand in the hope it would be shaken.

"Pol," said Apollo, shaking Bernard's hand with a firm grip that brought tears to his eyes as the bones seemed about to crumble. "Pol, like in Apollo," added Apollo, smiling as he released Bernard's hand.

Justin had second thoughts about offering a handshake.

"Like Apollo, the Greek god? Well, I have to say you look just like a Greek god," stated Bernard, thinking he was being flattering and complimentary.

"Thanks," Apollo responded with a wry smile. "I've been told that before."

Bernard was secretly pleased to hear that Apollo was Diana's brother. That left a door open. Could he possibly be gay, too?

"So, are you guys planning anything interesting here in Mykonos?" enquired Justin, seeking to bring the tone back to simple conversation before Bernard said something inappropriate.

"My sister would like to pay a visit to Delos. I'm just here to keep her company."

"We *both* have a special interest in Delos," said Artemis. "We'll take a boat over there tomorrow. Hopefully, it will be more peaceful than Mykonos Town."

"Oh, there will be hundreds of cruise passengers there, too," said Justin. "That's one of their routine overpriced excursions. Come see the archaeological ruins—as an organised excursion—for ten times the normal ferry price!"

Delos was certainly special to Apollo and Artemis; they were born there. Many millennia earlier, Leto, a Titaness, just like Metis, the mother of Athena, had typically been seduced by Zeus. When Hera discovered that Leto was pregnant as a result of Zeus' adultery, she cursed Leto never to set foot on any piece of land to give birth. However, cast adrift on a boat on the open sea, Leto was guided by Zeus's brother, Poseidon, to a floating island, unanchored to the seabed. The island was Delos, where the twins were born, raised, and survived Hera's attempts to destroy them. Eventually, Delos became attached to the seabed just 10km from Mykonos, and the twins were accepted as members of the Olympian dynasty—gods in their own right.

"And what about you two gentlemen? How are you planning to spend your time in Mykonos?" asked Apollo.

"Bars and clubs and nude beaches," laughed Bernard. "Soaking up the sun, partying and dancing the night away."

"I don't think my sister will be doing the nude beaches. Will you, Art?" asked Apollo, throwing a glance towards her. "She doesn't like men to see her naked."

Artemis glared at Apollo. That was too personal a comment for casual conversation with strangers, even if they weren't interested in women. For all Apollo knew, they might be bisexual!

"Art?" enquired Justin. "I thought you were called Diana?"

"Just a sort of nickname," said Apollo. "She's very arty. Takes great photographs."

"I take it not nude photos though," laughed Bernard. "How about portraits? You could get a great holiday pic of me and Justin in our best swimwear."

Apollo cringed a little at the direction the conversation was taking. Artemis was not known for her patience with men, and especially with any kind of sexual suggestion.

"I shoot wildlife," snapped Artemis coldly.

"Some great natural pictures on the nude beach," chuckled Bernard once more. "Maybe you could try shooting men!"

"I don't carry a gun," said Artemis, but "I'm pretty good with a bow and arrow."

"Dangerous lady!" Justin observed. "And how about you, Pol? Are you a photographer, too?"

"I have my artistic talents," he responded, "but I'm also deadly with a bow and arrow. We've been known to do a bit of hunting together."

"Well, in that case, we'd better stay on the right side of you and Diana," said Justin, smiling. "Wouldn't want any little arrows sticking in us, would we, Bernard?"

Bernard was still harbouring the hope that Apollo might be more interested in him than he was giving away. He probably just didn't want his sister to notice.

"We'll be going to Elia Beach tomorrow, Pol," said Bernard. "You're welcome to join us if you don't fancy the trip to Delos."

Artemis quietly fumed at the suggestion. If Apollo even considered doing it, he would be in big trouble.

"No, thank you, Bernard," said Apollo. "I am looking forward to accompanying Art to Delos tomorrow."

"That's a shame, Pol," said Bernard, with a disappointed pout. "We could have had a lot of fun together."

Apollo had humoured Bernard's suggestive conversation since arriving at the pool. Now, it was time to have some fun with him.

"Did you know, Bernard, if I *was* Apollo, the Greek god, I would have the oracular gift to foresee your future? Would you like me to tell you your fortune?"

"Really, Pol? No, I didn't know that. Please go ahead. Am I going to get lucky?" replied Bernard, smiling hopefully.

"Are you a gambling man, Bernard?"

"Not big time, but I'll do the odd bet or play cards for small stakes. Why? What do you foresee?"

"I see three minstrels at the beach," stated Apollo with authority.

"Three minstrels?" muttered Bernard. "What can that mean? Are they going to rip me off? Do I need to avoid playing cards with these minstrels?"

"Tomorrow, you will be a winner," added Apollo.

"Really? What will I win? Will it be big stakes?"

"You will win somebody's ass," said Apollo.

"Whay hey!" cried Bernard. "This guy has the gift, and he says my luck will be in tomorrow!"

Justin laughed loudly.

"I think Pol is playing a little game with you, Bern. Don't take it seriously, then you won't be disappointed when you come home alone with me tomorrow night."

Bernard secretly hoped that Apollo would be the one offering his ass when Diana was looking the other way.

Artemis smiled to herself. She knew Apollo was the god of oracles and never told lies. The Oracle's predictions were always a little obscure and open to interpretation, but she was interested in seeing what the next day might bring.

"Now, guys," said Artemis. "I'd like to read my book, so let's end this daft conversation and relax in peace. Enjoy the sunshine."

The men and gods glanced at each other in turn and smiled. Acknowledging the power of Artemis to shut them up, they all lay back to soak up the sun quietly.

Chapter 5: The Goddess of Lust

Aphrodite was the embodiment of sexual attraction. Notoriously known as the goddess of love, this was not the all-protective, undying love of a mother for a child. Nor was it the sense of wonder instilled by a beautiful scene, nor the awe inspired by an angelic voice accompanied by heavenly music. It was not the higher plane, radiant beauty emanating from Athena, with her love of correctness and justice. Nor the warm, motherly love of Hera, queen of the gods, a stateswoman, perfectly formed, her beauty demanding the worship of her superiority.

No! The love with which Aphrodite was associated was purely sexual: physical attraction, lust and passion. Aphrodite's beauty left screen goddesses way behind in her wake. Marilyn Monroe, Raquel Welch, and Brigitte Bardot were the mere serving girls of the queen of desire. Her beauty left men trembling at the knees while other parts stood to attention.

Enchantingly beautiful, blue-green eyes with intense, dilated pupils peered out from under long, dark, flickering eyelashes above a perfectly shaped nose and full lips, which pouted just enough to look as if they were asking to be kissed. She was a seductive vision. The fullness of her curves drew men's eyes to all of the features that defined her as an erotic female—an object of fantasy.

Aphrodite did not inspire love in men; she provoked lust. Not really an emotion, but more a desire for physical satisfaction, which might sometimes be equated with love at first sight. For a lucky few, such love might endure and develop into the strong emotional and intellectual bond of soul mates. However, such an outcome required no assistance from Aphrodite. More often, the fulfilment of lust would be followed by disillusionment and a gradual loss of interest.

She commanded Cupid's little arrows to strike at pining hearts. Sometimes, this was to help entwine destined lovers, but other times, to maliciously entrap unsuitable partners into doomed relationships.

Aphrodite was the firstborn of the Olympian gods, preceding even Zeus, their king, and his siblings. In fact, she hadn't been *born* in any normal sense of the word. She had congealed from the blood and semen which poured from the gonads of the sky father, Ouranos, after they had been severed and cast into the Aegean Sea by his son, the Titan, Kronos.

Her horrific creation took place in the ancient times before the emergence of the Olympian gods. From a grotesque scene of mutilation, Aphrodite had been sculpted into the ultimate beautiful creature. She had emerged from the waves, standing erect on a giant clamshell that washed up onto a beach near Paphos on the island of Cyprus.

She was called the goddess of love, but her own marital life was a soap opera threesome. Married to a genuine, caring lover, Hephaestus, with whom she shared her true devotion and parenthood of a child, she took every opportunity to betray him in crazy, passionate, lustful embraces with the god of war, Ares, his own brother.

Surely an unlikely relationship? Love and hate! Beauty and beast! Peace and war! It seemed that only the strongest anger and hatred could calm the hottest passion of Aphrodite, while only nature's most beautiful lover could sedate the violent nature of Ares.

Hephaestus was obliged to turn a blind eye to his unfaithful wife. He had tricked Hera into awarding the hand of Aphrodite as his prize in marriage. Although their mutual respect and friendship had blossomed, it seemed that he could only provide companionship and household comfort to Aphrodite. Her true, passionate desire would only ever be satisfied by Ares. Yet it seemed that neither Aphrodite nor Ares experienced the true love of soulmates: only intense passion and sexual release.

Today, Aphrodite glided slowly through warm Mediterranean waters, swimming a few feet below the surface. She liked to follow the multitude of small multicoloured fish, reaching to touch them with outstretched fingertips as she snorkelled in one of her long-time favourite haunts. Yellows, greys and fluorescent blues darted, twinkled and flashed in the sunlight as the fish turned and twisted in their effort to escape the giant but beautiful creature that pursued them.

Since the heyday of the Olympian gods, Aphrodite had liked to swim in the warm bays of southern Cyprus and sunbathe on her favourite beaches. She would amuse herself by people-watching, often deciding when to throw love's dice in the direction of young couples. However, in recent decades, the beaches and surroundings had changed beyond recognition from the peaceful paradise in which she had amused herself over the centuries.

Tourist developments had expanded into purpose-built towns of apartment blocks, hotels, beach bars, restaurants and souvenir shops. Gone were the beachside dunes, scrubby woodland and meadows which had once graced Cyprus's southern coastline. Now, ever more people were crowding the beaches, creating new vistas, sounds and smells.

Aphrodite swam into a shallow, sandy-bottomed bay at the edge of a small island just 50 metres from the shore at Nissi Bay. The landward edge of the island had a beach of soft, white sand, sheltered from the sea breeze by a large outcrop of porous limestone 100 metres long by 20 metres wide.

Nissi Bay was a popular, crowded beach playground near the resort town of Ayia Napa. From the mainland beach, the island could be reached across a shallow sandbar, which was thigh-deep for most people at its deepest point. The little island was a slightly less crowded haven away from the main beach, but the constant noise almost drowned out the gentle lapping of waves on the shores of what used to be Aphrodite's private suntrap.

Like Ursula Andress, walking out of the water in *Dr No*, the first James Bond film, Aphrodite rolled her hips and stretched her immaculately crafted limbs up the gentle incline of the sandbar. Clad in a scanty yet elegant pale bikini that accentuated the tan of her skin, she removed the diving mask and snorkel that had hidden her face and wrang the water from her long, blond locks. She turned to look disdainfully back towards Nissi Bay. What had it become?

Shouts and screams of children mingled with the deep bass and percussion sound of club music exuding from loudspeakers in the bars along Nissi Beach. Blue and white sun umbrellas stood to attention in regular ranks all the way along the sand. Hundreds of people lay on sunbeds below the blue and white: a small army ready to raid the bars, restaurants and hotels.

On one side of the island, a jetty had been constructed, now forming the access point for all manner of boat hire and water sports activities. A steady stream of customers walked in each direction across the sandbar, to and from the jetty. Among those were many who were crossing just to invade Aphrodite's personal beach.

Three young men, maybe in their 20s, carrying half-litre plastic glasses full of beer, were striding along the sandbar a few metres behind her. Fluorescent, multicoloured swimming shorts shouted loudly from white torsos, rapidly turning red with sunburn. Hair cropped short, red noses. Slightly tanned limbs, all with a number of dark grey-blue tattoos of incomprehensible patterns, like they'd been drawn by a chimpanzee with a serious hangover.

From off-shore, a cacophony of sound blaring from motors screamed at Aphrodite's ears. Vrooom, splat, bruummm, thump, vrrooomm, splash, and constant pounding as Jet Skis slapped the tops of waves, their drivers revving engines like racing motorbikes.

Speedboats and motor boats towing inflatable, giant bananas, or pulling parachutes ridden by screaming tourists. The breeze carried the stench of petrol fumes onto the shore: poison gas, creeping up the beaches to choke the entrenched sun-worshippers.

As she turned to walk towards where she'd left her beach towel on the sand, an unwelcome, high-pitched, wolf-whistle smacked Aphrodite's ear. She turned slightly, looking back towards the source of the sound on her left. The three overgrown youths, striped red and pink by the UV rays, grinned in her direction.

"Ya'ahright, luv?" said the one closest.

The goddess glanced in turn at each of the three, giving them a hard stare, like that of a strong-willed schoolteacher in response to insolent adolescents.

"I'm fine, thank you," she replied with a scowl.

"Wanna join us? Ya look like you could do with a bit o' dick."

The three laughed loudly at such brilliant wit.

Aphrodite looked at them in disgust. *Mancunians!* she thought. *Sound like Oasis. Not a brain between the three of them.* "You're more of a dick than I'd want to deal with," she replied.

The two companions guffawed at Aphrodite's put down of their friend, whose face now flushed with embarrassment, even more than it had been previously.

"Ah well, gorgeous," he added, trying to save face, "if ya change yer mind, ah'll be just over 'ere."

Ignoring the three men, Aphrodite walked to her beach towel and lay down. "Maybe I'll have to deal with those three," she said to herself. "I could make two of them fall madly in love with the funny guy, and make him fall in love with a seagull. That would cool their ardour." She smiled to herself.

"It's a shame all of these idiots are allowed to litter such a beautiful place with their presence," said a familiar voice from a figure who had quietly approached from the sandbar wearing a bikini and carrying a towel featuring a print of an owl.

"Athena!" she exclaimed. "It's been a very long time! Great to see you."

"Whoa, she's gotta sexy mate with 'er!" shouted the Salford joker from along the beach. "Come join us, girls."

Athena looked across to the group of lads.

"Who let the monkeys out of their cage, Aphrodite?" Athena said.

"Unfortunately, all sorts of idiots come here these days. The mortals need a good war to cull their numbers. I'll speak to Ares about that. Maybe he can make Putin push his little red button!" Aphrodite replied, then continued. "I was thinking about making them fall in love with a seagull, or possibly just turning them into crabs."

"That would be divine intervention, Aphrodite. You know we're not supposed to do that. It's against Zeus's code of conduct. I have a better way. Why not buy them a beer each? I have a little potion that is a very strong laxative. A few drops, and it'll hit within half an hour. They'll spend the next few days on the loo," said Athena, laughing.

Aphrodite smiled her approval. "Sounds like a good plan. One which Zeus would surely approve of. They're just the sort of yobs who would spike a girl's drink with something."

"Just watch, Aphrodite. I'm going to stop their nonsense."

Athena turned towards the lads. "What are your names, boys?"

"What? You gonna report us for somethin'?" said one.

"He's Tom, I'm Dick, and that's 'arry," said another, nodding to his friends in turn. "What about you, luv? What's your name?"

"I'm Athena, and this is Aphrodite," replied Athena.

"Ya think I'm fuckin' stupid or somethin', luv," said Dick, laughing as if he'd outwitted Athena.

"Strange you should say that," said Athena with a smile. "Look, guys, we're just trying to relax on the beach here in peace. So why don't you three just do the same? Maybe you'll meet some nice girls who'll be more interested in you at the pub tonight."

Tom, Dick and Harry all laughed loudly.

Athena turned to Aphrodite, saying, "I'm just off to get us some beers. Back in a few minutes." Then she stood up, strolled into the water and waded across the sandbar towards the main beach.

For a few very long minutes, the three tossed inane comments towards Aphrodite while she continued to ignore them. Eventually, Athena returned across the sandbar carrying two half-litre plastic glasses of beer.

"Oh, thanks, luv," shouted Dick. But there's three of us. You only brought two."

"If you were gentlemen, you'd offer to buy us the drinks!" replied Athena. Then she added, "Look, guys, if I give you these two beers, will you stop pestering us, please?"

"Sounds like an offer we can't refuse," said Harry.

"OK, then," said Athena, walking over to the lads.

"You can share these between the two of you. I'm not buying a third one," she added, passing the two glasses over to grabbing hands."

"Hey, Athena, are you crazy, giving them our beers?" said Aphrodite, supporting the ruse.

"Don't worry, Aphrodite. They'll leave us alone now. I can go get some more for us," said Athena, winking at her fellow goddess.

"Hey, gimme some o' that!" demanded Tom as Dick started to knock the beer back.

"OK, OK," replied Dick. "We'll share them properly."

"Daft bitch," added Harry. "Does she really think we'll be quiet now? We'll see about that," he sneered as he took a large swig of the beer.

Athena ignored the last comment as she strolled back across the shallow water to buy two more beers.

For the next few minutes, the lads were more interested in each getting their fair share of the two beers than in pestering Aphrodite. They were all well aware that such a beauty was a long way above their league. She would never look twice at any of them.

Athena returned across the sandbar again with two more beers. She passed one to Aphrodite as she sat down on her beach towel. They sipped the ice-cold drink and chatted, happy to be left in peace for a while. Athena explained her reasons for dropping in on Aphrodite as part of her mission to organise the Olympian reunion.

The loss of prestige and destruction of their temples was affecting all of the gods, not just Athena. This was obvious to Aphrodite, who was growing increasingly angry at the impact of tourism on her island of Cyprus.

"Of course, I'll join you in Athens," said Aphrodite. "Zeus will have to relent. We need to start intervening in human affairs if we're ever going to restore our authority."

"Hey luv, we've finished them beers. How about three this time?" said Dick from his spot on the beach a few metres away.

Aphrodite glanced at Athena with a concerned expression.

"Don't worry, Aphrodite," said Athena. "It won't take much longer."

Athena turned again towards the yobs.

"That's not what we agreed," said Athena. "You said you'd leave us alone if I gave you those beers."

"I never said that," argued Dick. "That were 'im," he said, indicating Harry.

At that moment, Tom butted in, "Hey, lads, ma gut's a bit off, ah think. Ah gotta go to't loo."

“Me too!” Harry added, clutching his abdomen as rumbling sounds became audible.

“Did ya spike our drinks, luv?” snarled Dick.

Athena shrugged her shoulders. “Why would I do that? Those were our drinks, and I gave them to you to shut you up. Anyway, if I’d put something in them, it wouldn’t have worked so quickly, would it? It’s probably something you’ve eaten from one of those beach bars. Not very hygienic over there: raw burgers sitting out in the hot sun and flies everywhere.”

What Athena said seemed to make sense. They had eaten burgers earlier, and now all three were starting to have serious gut cramps. Unable to continue the debate, they all rose from the beach and waddled as quickly as they possibly could with buttocks held tightly together. None of them could even risk the smallest fart!

The goddesses laughed as the three idiots minced their way across the sandbar. They wouldn’t be troubling anybody else for at least a few days.

Chapter 6: A Visit to Delos

Hector and Helen climbed up the gangplank of the Orca, the 135-foot motor launch which would take them on the 30-minute crossing from Mykonos Old Port to the jetty at Delos. The main deck was mostly enclosed accommodation, sheltering an interior lounge from the sea breeze and strong sunshine. However, it was a beautiful late spring day—not too warm to climb the steps to the uncovered upper deck. From there, they would have a clear view of the open sea and surrounding island rock formations and bays as they crossed the 10km from Mykonos to Delos. There were a dozen rows of seats arranged in three ranks, with aisles between them. Hector and Helen sat down on the port side, facing the back of the boat.

Their morning had been quite busy. Rising relatively early after their ship's arrival in Mykonos from Piraeus, they quickly took the lift from their deck four cabin up to the breakfast buffet on deck twelve. Helen grabbed a window table with a view across the gap between the ship and Mykonos Town.

Hector had joined the disorganised queues, searching for edible slices of bacon and not-too-rubberised eggs. He complemented them with bread rolls, coffee, and something vaguely resembling orange juice. Pushing past the growing number of breakfast seekers, he found his way back to Helen.

After breakfast, they returned to their cabin, where they dressed appropriately for their morning trip to Delos. They grabbed a few bits and pieces to stuff into Hector's satchel: the obligatory suncream, dark glasses, a water bottle and some items rescued from the breakfast buffet to make cold, processed meat and cheese rolls. Donning their sunhats, they headed down to deck three and joined a long queue of people waiting for the shuttle boats to take them to Mykonos Old Port.

Eventually, it had been their turn to swipe their ID cards as they left the deck interior, stepping out to a platform from which they were assisted onto the gangway to board a waiting shuttle boat. Once the shuttle was loaded to capacity, they were carried across 800m of bay to the dockside in the Old Port.

At the dock, they met with the tour guide, Nico, who had been reserved for their group of about 30 people by the cruise operator. Once Nico had gathered the group together, he gave a brief introduction and safety talk. Sunhat, sunscreen, drinking water, comfortable shoes, rounded off with, "Follow my little Greek flag, and stay in pairs, at least!"

The group then boarded the Orca.

Apollo and Artemis had breakfasted in the dining room of their hotel before walking around the waterfront to the dockside of the Old Port. There, they had bought return tickets to Delos for a fraction of the price the Johnsons were paying. Of course, they didn't have a tour guide, but they already knew more about Delos than any tour guide would.

From the dockside, the gods walked up a gently inclined gangplank and passed through an enclosed lounge to the stern, where they climbed the stairs to the open upper deck. They found seats in the middle aisle and settled among the crowd of tourists who were rapidly filling the boat. Unknown to them, Hector and Helen, who had encountered Athena just the day before, were sat across the aisle to their right as they faced the stern of the boat.

Within a few minutes, the banks of seats surrounding the twin gods had filled with tourists. The majority were smartly dressed American ladies or couples in their 50s, 60s and 70s. A fashion parade of designer sunglasses peered from under a variety of straw, canvas and cotton sunhats.

A jovial group of diverse Americans, black, white and mixed race, joked and laughed happily together as they discussed their cruise ship experiences. Artemis people watched, bemusedly, while Apollo studied the clouds, indifferent to the modern-day mortals sharing their mode of transport.

As the 11:30 departure time arrived, the crew untied the ropes securing the Orca fore and aft. Dock hands pulled the gangplank onto the quay while the boat crew closed the access gate. The engine tone raised a pitch, rumbling louder and exhaling thicker exhaust fumes. The helmsman navigated the boat out from between two other boats tied in front and behind the Orca at the dockside. Moving carefully away from the dock, the vessel turned slowly around, gradually increasing speed as it steered into the main channel towards the harbour exit.

Looking back towards the harbourside, Artemis took in the scene. Brightly coloured fishing boats bobbed gently at the water's edge beside a short pier. Splashes of red, white, black, and shades of blue contrasted with the rich golden brown of varnished decks and cabin panels. Beyond the boats, at the shore end of the pier, the little church of Agios Nikolaos of Madena stood proud. A shining mantle of whitewashed walls wearing a bright blue dome on top: the guardian of the fishing boat pier.

Along the waterfront, a multitude of tourists milled between cafes and souvenir shops, stopping for coffee, beer, mid-morning snacks, or simply browsing at the largely overpriced offerings of the waterfront tourist shops. The café fronts all sported dirty-white canvas canopies, shading their outside tables from the strengthening sun. Only a few business vehicles disturbed the waterfront tarmac: a handful of pickup trucks and vans, delivering to the shops and cafes or removing the debris of the previous day's tourism trading.

Behind the waterfront businesses, a small town of whitewashed buildings reached up the gentle incline on which Mykonos Town had been constructed. They were flat-topped, cuboid, white structures, like a randomly arranged pile of varied-size sugar cubes. The cuboid arrangement was occasionally punctuated by a church dome painted either blue or brick-red.

The buildings had been dropped into a nostalgic postcard arrangement—too close together to allow modern forms of transport to pass. Narrow alleys formed a maze interconnecting small squares or wider streets where restaurants had enough room to place their outside tables and the night people could party.

Hector stretched his legs as the Orca left the harbour, picking up speed as it turned westwards, heading between the moored cruise ship and the shoreline.

"Hey, look, Hector," Helen said, pointing back to the right. "It's them windmills you see in all the tourist info."

A row of six windmills formed a guard of honour along a headland at the southern end of the old town. Multi-armed white giants, each with a pointed cone of grey-brown roof on top, faced northeast towards the prevailing winds. The colourful cafes of Little Venice looked back at windmills from across a small bay.

"We could've saved a few dollars by just goin' down there for a beer or two today," complained Hector. "Instead of payin' an arm 'n' a leg to see some more old ruins."

Artemis's ears pricked up. Had she just heard somebody refer to her birthplace as "some more old ruins"? Athena would have been pleased to know that Artemis was forming a similar opinion of Hector to that she'd experienced the previous day.

"They're not just old ruins, Hector. There's 3000 years of history over there. "That's 2800 more than the US of A!" said Helen.

"We've got our own old ruins. Utah, Nevada, Arizona, New Mexico. Why do we need to see these ones?"

"Don't be a pleb, Hector. Delos was like New York City back before Rome was built. They controlled all the money and stuff being shipped around the Med."

"I'm not too keen on these ancient Greeks, Helen. That woman on the Acropolis terrified me yesterday."

"Oh, Hector. Don't start that again. You and your Athenian ghosts!"

Overhearing the conversation, Artemis smiled. That woman? Athenian ghosts? At the Acropolis? Could it be possible Hector had a close encounter with Athena?

The Orca motored out of the large bay that stretched across the western side of Mykonos, then turned southwest through a channel between two small islands, Kavouras and Baos, little more than large, rocky outcrops. On Baos, a 20-metre-high rock about 200m x 300m, there was a whitewashed church with a clay-red roof.

"Look at that, Helen!" laughed Hector. "A church on a rock out at sea! How the hell d'the congregation get to mass on Sundays? Noah's Ark?"

Even in the relative calm of an almost windless, late spring day, the waves crashed on the steeply inclined, jagged rocks around Baos. Surely any attempt to land there would be treacherous?

A tour guide explained that the island was used as a base by a pirate, Georgios Bao, in the 1770s to protect Mykonos from the ships of the Ottoman Empire who were colonising Greece. From the anchorage behind the rock, he would emerge to attack and loot their ships before they could raid Mykonos. The church was built later and was named the Church of St. George. The church and the island had both been named in honour of the pirate, George Bao.

"Well, wha'dya know?" said Hector. "I guess he was like a Mykonosian Robin Hood. It's a bit like havin' a Bishop Blackbeard!"

Motoring onwards towards Delos, the Orca crossed a 2km wide channel separating Mykonos from Delos. A Seajets fast ferry sailed past within about 200m, carrying a cargo of island hoppers to Paros or Naxos, each well under an hour from Mykonos on the fast catamaran travelling at 40 knots. A gushing jet of white water sprayed behind it as it passed, like the wake of a huge water skier. The Orca rocked back and forth as several waves from the wash of the Seajet hit it side on.

"Whoa, that was a big one!" yelled Helen.

"That's what all the girls say," responded Hector.

Artemis glanced at them disdainfully while a few of their neighbouring shipmates laughed loudly.

After crossing the shipping channel, the helmsman steered the tour boat around the rugged northern end of Delos. Steep, weather-battered rock faces of brown gneiss topped by grey limestone sheets suggested that Delos was another fortress island like Baos. However, as they continued into calmer waters between the small island and its very close neighbour, Rhenia, the landscape changed to undulating meadows that rolled down to the shore. In the past, they may have been pasture or arable fields.

The boat followed the coastline south for nearly two kilometres until the remains of the main Delos settlement, which once housed 20,000 inhabitants, became clearly visible. It swept up from the shoreline to the summit of Mount Cynthus, the high point of Delos. Approaching the ancient site, the boat veered left into a sheltered harbour, with a landing jetty big enough for up to 10 Orca-sized boats to reverse in and land their catch of tourists.

The Orca crew fastened the stern end to the jetty and lowered a gangplank at the rear exit from which the passengers could disembark.

Tour guides instructed their groups on return times in case any individuals got separated. A three-hour tour was scheduled, which was insufficient to have any real appreciation of an archaeological site nearly a square kilometre in size.

While the tour groups assembled with their guides, Artemis and Apollo bypassed them on the jetty, thereby accessing the gate before the boatload formed a queue.

Delos had been inhabited throughout the first millennium BC. Its position as a settlement with large natural harbours led to it being a trading hub and treasury for many independent Greek city-states, of which Athens became the most powerful. Most of the temples, plus administrative and commercial buildings, were constructed using local limestone, gneiss and granite during the second half of the millennium. Ornate statues and monuments were sculpted from marble and granite that had been quarried on the island of Naxos, some 30km to the south.

In the mid-millennium, the Greek city-states had cooperated, fighting together to defeat the Persians. The island operated as a multicultural freeport and had waves of migration from various trading communities around the Mediterranean. However, various factors impacted the longer-term prosperity of the island. A war between the Athens-led Delian League and a Peloponnesian alliance led by the Spartans, followed by the decline of Athenian power and the rise of the Roman Empire, resulted in the decline and eventual complete depopulation of the island of Delos. For nearly two millennia, the buildings were allowed to crumble until recent restoration during the late 20th century and early 21st century.

Today, the layout of the main settlement has been clearly defined, thanks to the work of the local restoration team. Pathways, floors and the outer walls of many buildings were repositioned and partially reconstructed. Between them, some columns and the remains of statues were placed in their original positions. Metal plaques were inscribed with the history of the most prominent buildings for the benefit of those visitors who weren't accompanied by a guide.

Near the boundaries of the ancient site were a new museum and a few small chalets for temporary occupation by the archaeological team.

Those arriving by sea were presented with a landscape of partially restored buildings that formed a patchwork of whites and greys, resting on a meadow of brightly coloured wildflowers. A blanket of white, yellow, blue and purple on a soft, green bed, across which the remnants of the Delos dwellings, temples, public buildings and monuments rested in an idyllic landscape of ancient peace. The site was big enough to quickly soak up the groups of tourists, who spread themselves thinly amongst the avenues, alleys and half-restored walls of ancient homes.

Apollo and Artemis strolled into the site from the harbourside entrance gate. They passed between columns surrounded by scaffolding, inscribed as being constructed in honour of Apollo by King Philip of Macedon. An adjacent avenue, the "Sacred Way," led into an area where the remains of buildings to either side were marked by plaques describing them as the Temples of Apollo and the Temple of Artemis.

"Our temples, Apollo," said Artemis wistfully. "Here, they sacrificed goats and prayed to us. For hundreds of years, we were worshipped from here. Now look. Just some blocks on the floor, a few partly rebuilt walls, bits of columns, mostly lying flat."

"At least people still come to see them, Sister," replied Apollo. "Isn't that worth something?"

"Most of them don't really care about what any of this represents. It's just an old place. Old buildings. This is how people lived two thousand years ago. For the tourists, it's just a day out somewhere different."

They strolled further along the avenue, past the Agora of the Italians, once a large, walled business area with shops, wells, and a marketplace. Beyond the Agora, five lion statues stood on pedestals, facing the "Sacred Lake." As if pretending to be a sixth lion, a 21st-century grey cat strolled down the avenue, one of many that had made Delos their hunting ground.

"Did you know, Apollo," said Artemis, "the Greek government pays English vets to come to Delos every year and castrate these beautiful cats?"

"It needs to be done, Sister. There are too many stray cats on the island. They're killing all the small mammals, birds and lizards which live here. Eventually, the cats would starve if there was no food left for them other than what the museum staff feed them. The cat population needs to be kept low."

"But why British vets? Can't a local vet do that job?"

"They say that the local vets will leave a few cats with their balls intact so that they will be guaranteed government-paid work the following year. Anyway, you're the huntress. The goddess of wildlife. Isn't it your job to control wildlife populations?"

"In an ideal mythological world," Artemis sighed.

"I suppose these cats aren't wild. Just stray domestic cats," suggested Apollo.

"All cats are wild," replied Artemis. "They just pretend to be domesticated in order to get fed by humans. It's easier than hunting. Requires less energy."

The gods wandered around the bed of the Sacred Lake and passed the museum, climbing gently towards a track leading to the top of Mount Cynthus. Halfway up, they passed a small building with a few characteristic Dorian columns standing erect. A plaque outside the building identified it as the Temple of Hera. From there, they had a panoramic view down over the whole archaeological site.

"This is just wrong," snapped Artemis. "How could they place a temple to Hera above those of Apollo and Artemis?"

"Ah guess that's 'cause Hera was queen of the gods, ma'am. She's got a right to be at the top of the hill."

Artemis turned in the direction of the comment, which was drawled in an American accent. Two familiar people were trailing well behind their guide, Nico.

Oh no, not him again, she thought to herself.

Hector continued, "Don't mean to be nosey, ma'am, but ah couldn't help overhearing. So, ah thought Hera's temple is up here where, bein' queen, she can look down on the other gods."

"But we, uh, I," Artemis almost stuttered out the words, angry that this person thought that it was fine for Hera to look down on her. Composing herself, Artemis responded, "Apollo and Artemis were born on Delos. This is their island. Hera tried to stop them from being born and sent a serpent to kill them. Why should she be allowed a temple on Delos at all?"

“Good point, ma’am,” replied Hector, “but it’s all jus’ fairy stories, ain’ it? None of them guys actually existed.”

“Then why did the ancients build the temples?” argued Artemis, beginning to feel like putting Hector in his place.

“Maybe the ancients were still trying to work out how the world works, Art,” said Apollo. “People like this gentleman know better these days.”

Apollo had thought it prudent to interrupt before Artemis lost her temper.

“That’s right, dear,” added Helen. “Those stories were all just good fun. We can look back and laugh at them, now that people know better. And we can look in wonder at what those people built in the past. Crazy that they could build magnificent temples in a place like this, just for non-existent gods.”

Artemis bit her lip and did her best to smile at Helen.

She just called me ‘dear’! she thought to herself. *If Apollo wasn’t watching, I’d turn these two into a pair of deer and then hunt them down!*

“Time we headed back down the hill, Helen,” said Hector. “We still got that amphitheatre and theatre district with the mosaics to get around, and we’ve lost our guide. We should leave this young couple to enjoy the old ruins.”

Apollo chuckled as he raised his hand a little to wave the Americans on their way. He could feel his sister's fury as she stood, poised silently like a lioness ready to pounce on a gazelle.

As Hector and Helen continued along the path around the hillside in search of their guided group, Artemis gritted her teeth, then said to Apollo, "Why do they make me so angry? I want to punish that man!"

Apollo laughed, "They're harmless, Sister. They were just making what they took to be honest comments. If you'd told them we know better because we're actually Apollo and Artemis, they'd have laughed at us."

From a nearby wall, a small voice hooted at the twin gods.

"I see you've met Hector and Helen," came the voice.

Turning quickly, Artemis noticed a little owl perched on a nearby wall.

"Athena!" she exclaimed. "We weren't expecting you. I thought you'd given me all the details in my dream. What brings you to Delos?"

Checking quickly that no mortals were in the vicinity, Athena dropped her disguise and transformed into the lady who had met Hector in Athens.

"Just passing by. I'm on my way from Cyprus to Naxos to talk to our aunties, so I decided it would be nice to say hello to my half-siblings en route. It's a long way for a little owl to fly—Cyprus to Naxos—particularly after diverting via Olympus!"

"Not just any old owl, Sister," said Artemis with a smile.

"I came from Olympus via Ukraine and Cyprus. Still nice to have a little rest every now and again," said Athena.

"Ah, you've spoken to Ares and Aphrodite, then," said Apollo.

"I have, and they'll both be joining us in Athens," Athena confirmed with a smile.

"So, what are you going to do about Hector, Artemis? I made him pee in his pants yesterday. I think he's wearing new ones today. Just gave him a little virtual bladder squeeze."

Artemis was shocked. "Isn't that divine intervention, Athena? That's supposed to be forbidden!"

"Yes, I know. But we need to intervene on a much larger scale if we're going to reinstate ourselves as gods. That's exactly why I want a forum with all the Olympians, to persuade our father, Zeus, that this is necessary."

"Well, you have my support, Athena. Certainly, when it comes to Mr. Hector, I'd like to teach him a little lesson, too," said Artemis. "Maybe I could do the rectal squeeze. That would quieten him down for a while," she laughed.

"That could be a bit unpleasant if you're sat near him on the boat back to Mykonos," noted Athena.

"True. Could be a bit smelly," said Artemis, adding, "I could make him and his wife fall asleep in a back alley behind the old Theatre Quarter ruins. Maybe nobody would notice them until they'd already missed their boat back to Mykonos?"

"But it'll be the last boat back today, so they wouldn't get to their cruise ship before it sails on to Santorini, or wherever it's stopping next. These cruise ships don't wait for missing passengers."

"Great! I'll do that then," said Artemis with glee.

"That would be a much more serious divine intervention than just making him pee himself," said Apollo. "He didn't harm you, Artemis. He just made a few comments you disagreed with. I don't think Zeus would approve," stated Apollo.

"Why do you have to be so sensibly boring, Brother?" asked Artemis, worried he was going to spoil her fun.

"Apollo's right, Artemis," Athena said. "Best to just leave them be and look forward to the day when divine intervention is no longer taboo. Hopefully, very soon."

"What's the plan then, Athena? When are you having your party in Athens?" asked Apollo.

"It's not a party!" Athena objected. "This is a serious matter. Deciding the future importance of the Olympian gods, Apollo!"

"Sorry, Sister," he added. "Just trying to keep it light."

"I'm off to Naxos now to speak with the ladies. Hopefully, they can catch a fast ferry to Athens tomorrow or the day after. You could join the boat in Mykonos, and we could all meet for dinner in the evening to plan for a more formal discussion."

"That should be fine with us," said Apollo. "Let us know what you agree in Naxos, and then we can join you on the boat to Athens."

"I'll be in touch later," said Athena, stepping behind a high wall.

A moment later, a little owl appeared on top of the wall, winked at the twins, and fluttered quietly off around the slope of Mount Cynthus in the direction of Naxos.

"So that's it then," said Artemis, sulkily. "I'm not allowed to humiliate these mortals."

"You don't need to, Sister. That would be beneath you. Just humour their stupid comments and remember you're heavenly and divine," advised Apollo.

The two descended to the bottom of an impressive Delian amphitheatre and then walked back through the Theatre

Quarter. A winding path took them through streets of ancient buildings that contained partially restored frescoes until they emerged near the jetty, where a line of tourists queued to reboard their boat.

Hector and Helen had caught up with their guide, Nico, and embarked on the Orca, ready to return to their cruise ship. Little did they realise how close their excursion to Delos had brought them to the gods who'd been born there thousands of years ago.

The rest of Hector and Helen's day would be uneventful. They would return to their floating hotel, followed by a cocktail, evening meal, and onboard dinner, remembering the day as just an expensive excursion to see some "old ruins."

Chapter 7: The Minstrels on the Beach

As Apollo and Artemis were heading off for their trip to Delos, Bernard and Justin were negotiating a day rate to hire an all-terrain quad bike. Happily agreeing on 60€ for a 300cc machine, they tied their beach bags to a rack behind the seats using elasticated bungees. With Justin in the driver's seat and Bernard behind, holding his waist, they set off through the busy morning traffic, ascending narrow winding roads through Mykonos Town, heading away from the old port area.

At the top of the town, they joined the main highway toward the airport, then climbed to a junction signposted for Ano Mera, the largest community town in the central part of the island. Although they felt a little vulnerable on their quad bike, the traffic outside Mykonos Town was light. They could relax and take in the scenery of the mountainous terrain as they passed through the fairly barren countryside 100m above sea level. Straw-coloured dry fields, with occasional patches of green, reached up the hillsides—a landscape dotted with white buildings that glowed brightly under the clear sky.

At Ano Mera, Justin looked for signposts to Elia Beach. Meanwhile, Bernard navigated on Google Maps from the rear of the seat while holding on precariously.

"Next right, then a bit further on, you take a left turn and follow the road south to the coast," instructed Bernard.

Justin smiled, confident he could read the road signs, but also reassured that he was going in the right direction. The road signs directed them, just as Bernard had described. After taking the left turn, they followed a narrower road along a hilltop for a mile or two, eventually descending down a fairly steep section. Winding down several hairpin bends, they arrived at the edge of the resort, down in Elia Bay. At the bottom of the hill, they turned right into a large car park, where they quickly found a space for the quad bike.

Turning towards the sea and scanning the beach from left to right, Bernard sighed, impressed by the scene before him.

"Isn't this absolutely gorgeous, Justin?" he said.

The arc of a 600m white sand beach crept around the azure water like a brightly lit crescent moon against a blue sky. For most of its width, the beach was planted with straw-topped sun umbrellas, each partially shielding a pair of wooden sunbeds. The sunbeds and umbrellas were laid out in regular, parallel lines, neat ranks, up to six rows deep between the sea and the back of the beach, looking like they were waiting for some terracotta army to come and relax in the sunshine.

Justin was less impressed.

"The sunbeds are too close together," he muttered. "And the beach is covered in them end to end. There's no room to lie on the sand if you don't want to pay their rip-off price for sunbeds!"

"Maybe the prices won't be that bad, Justin," said Bernard. "And we're here for the day, after all, so maybe it'd be worth having them."

"I don't need a sunbed, Bern. I'm happy to lie on a beach towel. This is just another way of squeezing money out of tourists. There are at least 3 to 400 umbrellas there. That's 6 to 800 sunbeds. They'll charge at least 50€ per pair of sunbeds here. That's €20,000 a day they're going to make. For what?!"

"Well, at least the car park was free," added Bernard.

"If they're full up two months in high season, and 50% full one month either side, then that's about 60 days at 20,000 plus 60 days at 10,000. That's nearly 2 million euros per season, just for hiring out sunbeds on one beach! And that's a conservative estimate. We're in the wrong business, Bernard."

"But just look at the colour of the sea and that nice soft sand, Justin."

"This will have been a beautiful beach, until the tourists discovered it and the con men arrived to exploit the tourists. Let's look for a spot to throw down our towels. They can stick their sunbeds," grumbled Justin.

As they looked towards the sea, the Elia resort was mainly on their left, at the eastern end of the beach. It was a holiday village of expensive resort hotels and exclusive rental properties, with a handful of bars, expensive restaurants, and tourist exploitation shops. The sunbeds in front of the village area were crowded, mainly occupied by families with children.

Moving westwards along the beach, away from the resort village, the mix of clientele changed noticeably. There were fewer and fewer families, couples, and ladies and more and more single men, male couples and groups of men.

"I did tell you this was the best gay beach on Mykonos, didn't I?" chuckled Bernard.

"You floozy, Bernard. That's why you were so keen to come here!"

As they strolled westward along the arrays of sunbeds, Bernard studied the bodies lined up, feet facing south towards the sea and the sun. Some face up, some face down, all men, all naked as the day they were born. All shapes and sizes, but most young, fit and beautifully bronzed.

"I just love this symmetry, Justin, face down, face up, face down, face up," he laughed, beginning to sing to a familiar tune.

"Bum, willy, bum, willy, bum, willy, bum, willy, bum, willy, bum, willy, bum, bum, bum, oh goodness gracious me!"

"Should I know that song?" asked Justin.

"Before your time. Peter Sellers and Sophia Loren. Goodness Gracious Me. You'll find it on YouTube."

At the far western end of the bay, they found a small, less crowded area beyond the end of the sunbed plantation.

"This'll do me," smiled Justin, spreading his towel and removing his Speedos in keeping with the other occupants of the beach.

Bernard did the same, all the while admiring the scenery around them.

"Stop staring at everybody, Bernhard. Some people may find you offensive."

"Can't help myself, Justin. I've never seen so many dicks in one place. I feel like a kid in a sweet shop!"

"Well, Mummy didn't give you any money to buy them, so it's better if you stop looking!"

"We're miles from the nearest beach bar here," noted Bernard. "You'll have to go and get the beers. My hands will shake too much walking back through this garden of Eden."

"I've got two beers from the hotel room fridge in my bag. We can have those while they're still cold," Justin replied, opening his bag and taking out two small cans of beer, which had been warming up for more than an hour since leaving the fridge.

"Well done, Justin; that'll do for starters."

They opened the beers and reclined on their beach towels, drinking them fairly quickly. It was now late morning and their thirst was increasing, along with the temperature. As he downed the last drop of his beer, Bernard opened his eyes widely in an expression of astonished surprise.

"Hey Justin, do you remember what that guy Paul said to me yesterday?"

"Which bit? Something about you being a winner?"

"He said I would win somebody's ass. But he also said something about three minstrels on the beach. Just look over there," said Bernard, nodding toward some men, settling onto the beach about 10 metres away.

Three well-built, bronzed, bearded men with quite long, scruffy hair were unfolding camping chairs onto the sand. They had the style of hippies, but all three were muscular and athletic in appearance. One of them looked quite elegant, cheeky and cheerful, seemingly the leader of the group. Another was a little smaller than the other two, had kind eyes, and walked with a limp. The third was a slightly dour-looking character with red but laughing eyes, as if he'd come straight from a party. There was something ambivalent about him, like he could be pleasurable company one minute, but could also make your life miserable.

The three had brought their own fold-up camping chairs and a variety of musical instruments: a guitar, a bouzouki, a mandolin, panpipes, and some sort of very old-looking percussion instrument—a tympanum—like a cross between a tambourine and a drum.

"Minstrels!" exclaimed Bernard. "They're going to do some busking on the beach."

"Buskers," grunted Justin. "Hopefully, they'll play something pleasant but loud enough to drown out the powerboats."

Justin nodded towards the pier in the middle of the bay, from which boat hire operators provided a range of very noisy motorboats and speedboats.

"You come to a beautiful beach where you just want to hear the waves breaking gently on the sand. But all you get is powerboats and the boom, boom, boom of beach clubs," he added.

"Oh, you're such a misery, Justin," said Bernard. We're here now. Let's just enjoy it. I'm lovin' every minute so far."

A short distance away, the three musicians had begun tuning their instruments. The man with the party eyes breathed gently through the panpipes, one note at a time. The guy with the limp gently plucked a guitar string while the band leader alternately plucked a bouzouki or mandolin string until all were harmonically aligned. Then they began to play.

Bernard and Justin had been expecting a little bit of background strumming, plucking and whistling—maybe melodic, maybe not. They didn't really mind, as anything would be better than the powerboat noises. However, what drifted to their ears across a very short stretch of beach was unlike anything they'd ever heard before.

A strangely ethereal, beautiful blend of bouzouki melody accompanied by slow, haunting tones from the panpipes, backed by gently strummed guitar, played to an unusually hypnotic beat. After a musical introduction of two or three minutes, the band leader breathed deeply and then began to sing.

Bernard and Justin both felt the hair on the back of their necks rise as they were almost emotionally overcome by an angelic rendition of what sounded like an ancient, tragic love song. Holding back tears, they listened intently, forgetting all of the other sights and sounds around them on Elia Beach.

For several minutes, the band continued to play until the song finished, and the final bar was closed by a panpipe note fading out into silence.

Excited and emotional, Bernard could not stop himself from applauding loudly. “Bravo, bravo, gentlemen. That was absolutely beautiful!” he exclaimed.

“Thank you,” replied the band leader with a smile.

An open guitar case lay on the ground, close to the musicians. People from a number of neighbouring sunbeds had already approached the case and deposited euro notes within. Justin strolled over to the group and dropped a 20€ note into the collection.

“Lovely tune, guys,” he said. “Is that a local folk song?”

“It’s a very old song about a god, cuckolded by his brother with his wife, the goddess Aphrodite,” said the guitarist with the limp.

“My, my, it’s no wonder it sounded so sad,” said Justin.

“Makes me cry, too,” said the guitarist.

The three looked up at Justin, smiling, and then red eyes played a short pipe sequence, which was the intro to the next song in their repertoire. Justin bowed his head in respect to their musicianship, then returned to his beach towel.

For the next hour, the two friends listened in wonder while the trio played the most beautiful music they’d ever heard. Sometimes swapping instruments and adding the tympanum or mandolin, they created an atmosphere which pervaded the surrounding beach. It almost seemed to declare:

"This music is Greece. It was here before you tourists. It was here when there were just the musicians. No sunbeds, no power boats, no beach bars. Just this magical bay and the sea, making their own music."

As they had been mesmerised by the captivating music, Bernard and Justin had moved a few metres closer to become the front row of the audience. When the musicians eventually took a break, Bernard decided it was time for introductions.

Addressing the three, Bernard opened the conversation. "That was fantastic music. Have you guys been playing together for a while?"

The band leader smiled and said, "We go back a few years together. We're all close relatives. We like to play old Greek traditional music."

"It really was beautiful music, and you've got a fantastic voice for those songs," Bernard said in an attempt to be complimentary.

"Can we offer you a drink? You must need some refreshment after entertaining us all with your music," added Justin.

"Thank you, gentlemen," said the band leader, "but we have our own refreshments with us. My friend here is a wine producer on the island of Naxos, and he has brought some special drinks for us," he added, indicating the red-eyed panpipe player.

"I'm Bernard, and this is my friend Justin. We're staying near Mykonos Old Port.

"Hi, Bernard," said the band leader, guessing Bernard wanted an introduction to the band.

"I'm Herm, this is Dion, and he's Feisty," he said, nodding first to red eyes and then to the limping guitarist.

"Feisty? He's trouble, is he?" asked Bernard.

"No, that's irony," replied Herm. He's actually the most laid-back of the three of us. But Feisty is easier to say than Hephaestus."

"Hephaestus?" asked Justin. "Like the Greek god?"

"Exactly like that!" replied Dion.

"And Herm is from Herman?" asked Bernard.

"No, Hermes," replied Hephaestus.

"Hermes?" asked Justin. "Like the Greek god?"

"Exactly like that!" replied Dion.

"And I guess Dion is Dionysus?" asked Justin. "Like the Greek god?"

"Exactly like that!" replied Dionysus.

Bernard laughed loudly. "Ha, ha, ha! You see what these guys are doing, Justin? They're pretending they're Greek gods. Sort of role-playing, like the human statues you get around the London Eye."

"Or actors," added Justin.

From among the instrument cases, Dionysus fetched a gourd bottle and three very traditional-looking pottery goblets, which he then filled with some of the contents of the gourd. He passed a goblet to each of his companions, who both drank a large mouthful, which they appeared to savour silently. They closed their eyes and seemed to focus inwardly, breathing slowly as if in meditation before eventually swallowing the liquid.

"That was a good year, Dion," said Hephaestus.

"Every year is a good year for my elixir, Feisty," replied Dionysus.

"They really do this Greek god act very well, don't you think, Justin?" said Bernard.

"That's how they get so much money dropped into the collection case, Bern. It's not just for playing the music. They're playing the part!"

"That must be very special wine, Dion," said Bernard. "Or maybe it's some sort of absinthe? You guys were certainly savouring it like it was much more than just fermented grape juice."

Dionysus stared at Bernard for a few moments, then smiled and said," All my wine is special. Maybe you'll have a chance to taste some before you leave Mykonos."

Bernard felt a little uneasy. Maybe it was Dion's hangover eyes, which seemed to stare straight through him. It was hard to decide whether he was trying to be friendly or if there was some veiled threat in his words. Deciding to change the subject, Bernard turned back to Hermes.

"Hey, Herm," said Bernard, "you know what's really strange? A guy at our hotel told us we'd meet three minstrels on the beach today. Paul, his name is. Said he can foresee the future, like Apollo the god."

"Do you mean Pol? Quite tall and muscular, with blond hair? Wears a laurel wreath pendant?" asked Hermes.

"Yes! That's him. He was with his sister, Diana," replied Bernard.

"Diana? Quite slim? Short, dark hair, tom-boyish cut?" asked Hephaestus.

"Yes! You know them?"

"Apollo and Artemis. We go back a long way."

"More close relatives?" asked Justin.

"Yes, how did you know?" asked Hermes, looking surprised.

"Are you one of these Greek gods fan clubs? You dress up and get together for conventions? Like Trekkies?" asked Justin.

"Trekkies?" enquired Dionysus.

"Star Trek fans," replied Bernard.

The three musicians looked at each other and laughed knowingly.

Bernard glanced down at the guitar case, which had been well-lined by euro notes, dropped by the many people who'd been sunbathing in the vicinity or just passing along the beach. Remembering what Apollo had said about being a winner today, he grabbed the moment.

"Do you guys play cards, by any chance?" asked Bernard.

"I've been known to have the odd little flutter," replied Hermes. "Why do you ask?"

"Well," sighed Bernard, "when I spoke to Paul, er Apollo, yesterday, he suggested I was going to have a lucky day today. I couldn't help noticing that you gentlemen were rewarded with quite a lot of money for playing so beautifully to entertain us. While you deserve every cent of that, I just wondered whether you would like to have a little card game to see if we could win some of that money from you?"

"Maybe we'll beat you," Hermes pointed out. "We wouldn't like to win all your holiday spending money."

"We'll be careful. We can limit the size of our stake. But Apollo said I'd be lucky today."

"Well, that worries me. They say Apollo always tells the truth. So maybe we'd be risking our earnings if we accept," added Hermes.

"Hey, guys," interrupted Justin, "Pol can't really predict the future. You don't know who's going to win. Can we afford to lose our spending money, Bernard?"

"But Pol was right about the three minstrels on the beach, so maybe he'll be right about me winning too."

"If he knows these guys, then he probably knew they'd be on Elia Beach today. He's trying to trick you into this card game," warned Justin.

Bernard turned away from the musicians to talk privately to Justin.

"I'll take the risk, Justin," said Bernard, adding in a whisper, "He didn't mention money. He said I'd win somebody's ass. So, I'm very curious."

"You slut, Bernard."

Bernard turned back towards the three musicians.

"OK, Herm. I'm happy to risk half of our holiday fund. Five hundred euros per player in the bank. Are you up for that?"

Hermes smiled at each of his fellow gods, then turned to Bernard.

"We don't play cards on the beach, but if you would like to risk your money, we could meet in Mykonos Town this evening. Then I'll bankrupt you!" Hermes declared, laughing.

"Well, that's a challenge, then," replied Bernard. "Just name the time and place, and we'll be there."

"Don't be crazy, Bern," said Justin. These guys are great musicians and great actors. Maybe they're great card players, too. We won't have enough money for the rest of our holiday if we lose."

"Remember what Pol said. It's my lucky day. Don't worry; I'll limit my stake. You can do the same if you're going to join in."

Justin sighed in frustration. What had Bernard got them into?

"The Glorious Bar at 9:00 this evening," declared Hermes. "It's a comfortable little bar with reasonably priced drinks, interesting cocktails, good meze food, and pleasant music. Just a street or two back from the Old Port.

"We'll be there. I'll look forward to enjoying my winnings," said Bernard, licking his lips.

"I think I need a beer," said Justin, "or probably something stronger! I'm off to the beach bar. Lager, Bern?"

"Yes, please, Justin. Thought you'd never ask."

"And now, gentlemen, we're going to play some more music," said Hermes.

The minstrels picked up their instruments and began playing once more, serenading the nearby sunbathers for another hour.

Bernard and Justin relaxed and listened in wonder, sipping their beers, soaking up the sun and occasionally waddling into the sea to cool off.

In the late afternoon, the time came to pack up and return to the hotel to clean up and prepare for the evening.

"Thank you for the music, guys," said Bernard to the three minstrels. "It's great to see how much money you've made. It'll be a great pleasure to win some of that from you later," he added, laughing.

"The pleasure will be all ours," said Hermes with a friendly smile.

Hephaestus gave a waving salute while Dionysus took another mouthful of his elixir.

"I'm really quite excited about tonight, Justin," said Bernard as the two strolled back to their quad bike.

Chapter 8: The Taverna Ladies

Along the southwest coast of Naxos, a calm Aegean Sea lapped gently against a ten-mile-long series of white sand beaches, occasionally fragmented by rocky headlands and cedar groves. Over the years, many clusters of hotels, tavernas, apartment blocks and holiday clubs had been developed on a one-kilometre-wide strip of land along the coast behind the beaches.

At the end of one long section of beach was a cedar grove overlooking a rocky outcrop of weather-smoothed granite that enclosed a few small, sandy coves. Above the outcrop, a whitewashed church not much bigger than a small family apartment sat on a low hill, proudly flying the Greek national flag. The beach was lined by a long fringe of sand dunes. Growing sporadically between the dunes, tamarisk trees, with grey-green, feathery leaves and boughs that spread almost horizontally at head height, provided islands of shelter from the summer sun along the shoreline.

A hundred metres along the beach from the little church, the Taverna Ambrosia offered an idyllic repose for bathers and sun-worshippers seeking food or refreshment.

Split into two by a minor road running along the coast, the front half of the taverna's terrace sat among the sand dunes at the edge of the beach. Two dozen sage-green-painted wooden tables were placed directly on the sand, just ten metres back from the lapping waves. A pair of tamarisk trees stretched above most of the tables, providing shelter from the sun in high season.

In the heat of the day, beach-goers would sustain themselves with hard or soft drinks, cocktails, coffee and light meals or snacks. Low-level, piped bouzouki music accompanied the gentle brushing of the waves across the sand, mixing with the sounds of children playing in the shallows. Beyond the beach, as the afternoon drained into evening, the sun would soon sink through a rapidly rusting sky before hiding behind the neighbouring island of Paros, less than ten kilometres away to the west, on the other side of a busy shipping channel.

Across the road from the beachside tables, the taverna was fronted by a crazy-paved terrace, housing another two dozen tables. Above the tables, a wooden frame supported a canopy of tamarisk branches over the outer tables, and a bamboo ceiling over the inner area. On the dining tables sat little bottles of olive oil and balsamic vinegar, accompanied by salt and pepper dispensers. At the back of the terrace, a blackboard was mounted on an easel, displaying chalked descriptions of “Today’s Specials”.

Just behind the dining terrace sat the Taverna Ambrosia. It was an unassuming building, painted a faded cream-white, with pale blue shutters pinned back beside each window. The lower floor comprised an indoor dining room, kitchen, guest toilets, reception and private business rooms. The private rooms used by the taverna’s owners were located on the upper floor. An annexe behind the building acted as a small apartment block containing accommodation for up to about twenty tourists.

The garden around the taverna was a rich blaze of coloured shrubs. Purple, pink, red, and white flowers of bougainvillea, jacaranda, hibiscus, oleander, and jasmine, the latter of which diffused an intoxicating, almost seductive perfume around the dining area. The scent mingled with mouth-watering aromas emanating from the kitchen.

Sometimes meats, other times seafood were barbequed in marinades or fried in olive oil, usually with garlic, onions and some spices, but always with herbs: oregano, basil, and thyme. And freshly baked bread, too. The kitchen baked their own bread to accompany their delicious fare.

“The best bread in Naxos!” some guests had been heard to declare.

Nobody could remember how long the current proprietors had been running the Ambrosia. Most were too polite to ask. They were two ladies of an age that was hard to define—somewhere between 30 and 60. They had ageless auras and were elegant, attractive and mature. They were welcoming and polite, mysterious but somehow anonymous, yet it was well-known locally that their cuisine was very special. Apparently, nobody had ever complained; they just marvelled at what they had been served.

Like most of the others on the island of Naxos, the taverna opened in mid-spring, around the end of April. It closed at the end of October every year when the tourist season finished. The two ladies were often the subject of speculation. A lesbian couple? Maybe. Maybe not! Sisters? Maybe. Maybe not! It seemed that one, Hess, played the role of hostess, while the other, Demi, was more concerned with food production. They were assisted by a third, probably younger lady, Perse, who it was thought was Demi's daughter. Perse was regarded as a bit odd. She was never seen during the winter months but showed up every spring looking rather pallid, unlike Hess and Demi, who always shared the bronzed glow that was standard among most Greeks.

It was assumed that Perse passed the winter in a northern country where she spent all her time indoors. At the start of the season, her hair and eyes were always dark, and her skin pale. Red lipstick emphasised a very "Gothic" complexion. However, by the end of the season, in the autumn, she had become almost natural-looking, skin reasonably tanned, long, dark hair sun-bleached. Most people were too polite to ask questions about the mysterious young assistant at the Ambrosia.

The three worked in perfect harmony as a team. Hess welcomed guests, showing them to free tables and delivering menus to anybody who'd already sat down. Together, Hess and Perse took orders. Demi did the lion's share of food preparation, while Hess assisted with presentation. Hess and Perse served plates and cleared tables together. At busier times, an additional person, a bearded man, Dion, apparently a relative who always looked a bit hungover, would join the three. Dion's priority was serving drinks, but all supported each other wherever there was a role in need of an extra pair of hands.

Today, late afternoon in the early holiday season, only a few tourists sat at the beachside tables. It was too early in the day for the evening dinner rush. The three ladies were sitting having a drink together at the edge of the dining terrace when a familiar, high-pitched hoot drifted towards them from the cedar grove.

"Whoo-whoo, whoo-whoo?" asked Athena.

"We all know whoo, Athena," replied Hess. "Little owls don't normally hoot in mid-afternoon. It can't be anybody else."

A very human-looking Athena strolled out from the cedar grove close to the taverna.

"Good afternoon, Aunt Hestia, Aunt Demeter, Cousin Persephone," she said, smiling. "How are you all?"

Hestia, the hostess, was the goddess of the hearth. She represented the importance of the homestead, the focus around which families and extended families would gather to dine, tell stories, listen, and generally consolidate the bonds that held their communities together. Hestia personified hospitality.

Demeter was the goddess of fertility of the Earth, of agriculture and production, responsible for the seasonal growth of the foodstuffs on which humanity relied for existence. She had once gone on strike when Hades, the god of the underworld, abducted her daughter Persephone and carried her off to be his bride. When all plant growth stopped, and the resulting famine threatened to destroy all life on Earth, Zeus persuaded Hades to release Persephone. However, Hades tricked her into eating six pomegranate seeds before returning to the upper Earth. As a result, she was obliged to return to Hades for six months every year. During the time Persephone is with Hades, Demeter mourns, and the plants stop growing until she returns.

Persephone is the queen of the underworld: the bride of Hades. She returns to be with her mother for half of the year, but she loves her husband Hades, even though he kidnapped her and took her to the underworld! So, she returns to him happily every year to rule the domain of the dead.

All three smiled in greeting, happy to see their wise relative.

"All the better for seeing you, Athena," Demi replied. "We haven't got Dionysos with us today. You can fill in as wine waiter and dishwasher this evening," she added, laughing.

"Gods serving dinner to mortals? Whatever is the world coming to?" demanded Athena in exasperation.

"You must have had a very tiring flight, Athena," said Hestia. "Come. I'll show you to a guest room where you can freshen up, then join us here. We've got so much to talk about."

"Thank you, Hestia. That will be most welcome," Athena replied with a smile.

After a short time, Athena returned to the dining terrace, eager to talk to the taverna ladies. Having passed through several centuries of immortal activities since their last meeting, Athena chatted for an hour or so with Hestia and Demeter to catch up. Persephone joined them when she could, in between serving drinks or clearing tables beside the beach.

Eventually, diners began to arrive for evening meals—mostly couples, but a few groups of four. Outside the school holidays, the visitors were usually all adults, intent on enjoying each other's company in an atmospheric, romantic setting.

For an hour or two, on either side of sunset, the gods fed and watered mortal men and women. The restaurant guests marvelled at the food that melted in their mouths and stunned their taste buds into submission to a wealth of flavours, all washed down by the tastiest wines they could remember. Little did they realise, but the music that floated around the tables was a recording of Apollo, Hermes, Dionysos and Hephaestus singing beautiful harmonies to traditional instruments.

"Best to make sure they drink plenty of wine," said Hess. "If their memory is a bit blurred, then they'll just remember having a very enjoyable meal. Otherwise, any Tripadvisor reviews will sound like bullshit, or people may think we're writing our own reviews."

Soon after 7:30, the azure blue sky was already fading into a paler tone. Across the water, Paros lost its detail, becoming a dark silhouette against a pale, orange-grey sky. The sun slowly dissolved into the horizon, all of its heat leaking across the skyline, turning it a darker orange, veering towards red. As the sky above blackened and the stars began switching on, the last hints of colour faded, and the horizon gradually disappeared. Only the distant street lights of villages dotted along the Paros shoreline remained visible.

At the taverna, a couple of dozen guests enjoyed their evening meal on the dining terrace, illuminated by the soft lights that decorated the wooden frame of the terrace canopy.

The quality of the food and wine, combined with the ambience in the Ambrosia restaurant, tied the diners to their tables. Like Odysseus's men in the Land of the Lotus Eaters, they remained, enjoying the moment, hoping it would last forever.

At the end of the evening, Hess and Demi had to persuade the last diners it was time to close up and explain that they would be welcome to return anytime the restaurant was open.

After clearing the last few tables, the goddesses settled down at one of them to continue their catchup.

“I couldn’t keep doing this service for mortals,” admitted Athena.

“We’re used to it, “said Hestia. “There’s something satisfying about making people happy.”

Athena tried hard to understand the sentiment but felt that it was demeaning for immortals to be serving ordinary, sometimes very ungrateful, people.

“What is it that brought you to Naxos, Athena?” asked Demeter.

Athena hesitated before answering. She could tell that Hestia and Demeter were content with the life they had, although immortality would always mean that their lifestyle must change alongside the future progress of the society in which they lived.

“I’ve been watching over Athens for a long time. I’ve seen the temples built, the people worship us, the people’s politics and beliefs change, and the temples destroyed. People now visit the Acropolis as though it was an ancient amusement park.”

How could she explain this to the taverna ladies?

“The thing is,” said Athena,” Zeus forbade us from divine intervention, but without it, people simply don’t believe we exist. The old temples are just artefacts of an earlier civilisation. Modern people have no respect for the Olympians, nor for the reasons the ancients built those temples. I want to organise a meeting of the Olympians so that we can all talk to Zeus together and decide whether we need to do something to reinstate our authority."

"You mean to ask Zeus to permit divine intervention?" asked Demeter.

"Maybe," confirmed Athena. "If that's the consensus among the gods."

"So, are you asking us to come to Athens or Olympia?" added Hestia.

"It's best to go to Athens. Then all the gods can see the things I've seen and maybe discuss the experience of the other Olympians. I can't be the only one feeling the frustration of being unable to influence how people behave."

"So, what should we do? Appear as gods in public?" said Demeter, "Strike people down for offending us? Give nice people special powers so that they can be nasty to bad people? I'm not sure what you're suggesting, Athena."

"I'm only suggesting that we all get together and discuss how we should deal with this. Do we just sit back and become increasingly unimportant?"

"We don't see anybody in the underworld until they're already dead," observed Persephone. "A bit too late for divine intervention!" she noted.

"All of your opinions are important," said Athena. "That's why I wanted to ask the gods to get together. Then we can come to a consensus on how we should behave in the future."

Hestia stroked her chin, reflecting on what Athena had said. "I'm not sure I really have anything to contribute, Athena," she considered. "How many temples of Hestia are in ruins?"

"I don't know," Athena responded. "Can't you tell me?"

"The point is," noted Hestia, "there aren't any."

Hestia let the point sink in with Athena before continuing.

"I am the goddess of the hearth—the focus of the homestead. People have always worshipped me around their campfires or in their homes. They didn't build large temples to me because I'm not a city; I'm their fireplace. They thank me for their meals around their own dinner tables, not in a large public place."

"But they don't pray to Hestia! They've forgotten you. They offer Grace to somebody, but is that you?" asked Athena.

"It doesn't matter. They are thankful for whatever they have in their homes. That is what I have always represented," Hestia replied, adding, "I am also the goddess of hospitality. It is important to welcome a stranger and provide for his or her needs."

"Exactly so," added Demeter. "Here at the taverna, we don't ask to be worshipped, but together, we welcome strangers. We do what we can to make them feel welcome and to provide them with the best possible service."

"But they are mortals, and you are gods!" Athena exclaimed. "Shouldn't they be serving you? Not the other way around!"

"Between Hestia and myself, we provide the hearth and produce. We offer hospitality without expectation in return. Hopefully, mortals can learn from us. They should respect what they have and be happy to offer something of that to anybody else in need. We are trying to set that example," Demeter asserted.

"Maybe there are no temples to Hestia and few to Demeter," said Hestia, "but just 10km from here, in the direction of Mount Zas, the highest mountain on Naxos, is the Temple of Demeter."

"Oh yes, "added Demeter, "my very own local ruin. It's not crowded like the Acropolis in Athens, but it is just another archaeological site. Many tourists come to visit and admire the temple, which is set on a hilltop, with beautiful views of fertile countryside and mountains all around. It's one hundred years older than the Parthenon."

"So, Athena, it seems that myself and Demeter don't feel so strongly about a trip to Athens," Hestia said. "Yes, it would be good to see all the Olympians again, but we're not too far from Apollo and Artemis when they come home. Persephone is our link to Hades. Poseidon is all around us. Dionysos serves our wine. We don't really need Aphrodite and Ares. Hephaestus is always welcome. Zeus and Hera are our siblings. They can visit if they want to, as long as Zeus can remember which one is his wife!"

"I'd be happy to join you in Athens, Athena," Persephone butted in. "Of course, that's assuming Mother and Hestia don't need me here?"

"I suppose you don't get many chances for a party down under, my dear," said Demeter. "After ten thousand half-years in the underworld, a trip to Athens might bring some colour to your face."

"I'm guessing we'll lose Dionysos too when you go. There's no way he'll miss out on a possible party!" said Hestia.

"I'm not organising a party!" said Athena, exasperated at the idea. "This is supposed to be a serious reunion to discuss our future as over-seers of humanity."

"I can join the discussion on behalf of the underworld," said Persephone. "You know Hades never leaves home. He won't go to Athens. He hasn't left the underworld since he came up to kidnap me ten thousand years ago. If we happen to have a post-discussion party, then I'm sure nobody will mind. I think Dionysos, Hermes and Apollo will all be more likely to attend if they think there's going to be a party afterwards," she added, laughing.

"Well, Daughter," said Demeter, "myself and Hestia are Olympians. We can easily summon a couple of secondary gods or sea-nymphs to stand in for you and Dionysos for a couple of days."

"Athena, we respect what you are trying to do," Hestia said. "We know you're concerned for all of us, not just for the Parthenon. Just what sort of divine intervention will put humanity on a straight and narrow path is a mystery to me. I wish you success in this venture, but I know both myself and Demeter are content with demonstrating what hospitality means to a mortal audience. Hopefully, some of them will learn from it."

Demeter added, “At least in the present, Hestia and I don’t have to deal with wars or famine. We live in an idyllic setting and have an enjoyable lifestyle surrounded by people who are generally enjoying themselves. If we were to attend your discussion, you would probably find our contribution a bit negative. You need to hear broad opinions, but I think you would resent us for not supporting you.”

Athena considered the points made by Hestia and Demeter. She needed consensus, not just mutual agreement.

“I’m sure you could have argued against me in a group discussion, if that’s how you felt, but I can accept it if you don’t want to join the trip to Athens. You can always pass your opinions in writing via Persephone so the other Olympians know how you feel. I may be annoyed by the tourists at the Acropolis, but I’m supposed to represent justice, and that means I need to listen to balanced arguments, even if they don’t agree with my opinion.”

“So how are we getting to Athens, Athena? “asked Persephone. “Can we just materialise there, or do we take a ferry?”

“Well, until we get the nod from Zeus, we have to live like mortals. That means we take a ferry. If we leave from here, we can pick up Apollo, Artemis, Hephaestus, Hermes and Dionysos at Mykonos. Aphrodite, Ares, Zeus and Hera will join us in Athens. Poseidon will probably just rock the boat without coming on board," said Athena.

"That sounds great!" said Persephone. "Such an opportunity to have fun away from all those dead people. Athens will be the opposite of the underworld."

"Please take this seriously, Persephone," added Athena, sounding exasperated. "How do I get through to you all that this is about the future of the Greek gods?"

"Even if you're discussing the future of the gods, that shouldn't stop you from having a little bit of pleasure in each other's company, Athena," added Demeter. "So, why don't you just be our guest for a day? You can relax on the beach. Swim with the fish in the sea. Enjoy our food and hospitality. For one day, you can live in our little bit of paradise and forget all about divine intervention. Then, when you do get back to Athens, you'll have had a chance to relax and think about it all with a clear head."

"Wise words, Aunt Demeter. I would love to stay here and enjoy your hospitality. Thank you."

"And now it's getting very late," observed Hestia. "Even us goddesses need some beauty sleep. It's time we retired for the night. Then Athena can have a nice, relaxing time tomorrow."

"Thank you, all, for making me so welcome. Even if you don't agree with my reasons for visiting you," said Athena. "Good night, ladies. Sleep well."

Athena returned to the guestroom, where she transmitted a few short telepathic messages; the first one was to Artemis.

"Will be on Seajet from Naxos, arriving Mykonos, 11:45, day after tomorrow. Hope you can all join me on boat from Mykonos. Sleep well. Love Athena."

Then to Aphrodite:

"Arriving in Piraeus, 14:50, day after tomorrow, with the gods and goddesses. See you on Areopagus Hill, 16:00."

And finally, to Zeus:

"Olympians meeting, 16:00, day after tomorrow at Areopagus Hill. Love, Athena."

She then dropped into a deep sleep.

Chapter 9: A Game of Poker at Glorious

After their trip to Elia Beach, Bernard and Justin showered and dressed in casual shirts and shorts for the evening. They left their hotel very early and strolled around the bay of the Mykonos Old Port. Trotting along the fine sand of the Choras Mikonou Beach, they chatted about their experience earlier in the day at Elia Bay and their prospective card game.

"Apollo says I'm a winner today!" chuckled Bernard.

"Careful, Bern. These guys are probably con men—out to catch daft tourists like you and me. Don't get too excited, and be careful how much you risk."

"Lighten up, Justin. It's all part of the fun. Con men don't play music like that. They may be very good entertainers, but I think they're professional artists acting out roles, not bad guys."

"Or professional hustlers, Bern!"

They climbed a few steps at the end of the beach and walked along a short path leading onto a wide promenade that skirted the old port area. Restaurants and bars lined the town side of the promenade—two and three-storey, whitewashed, cuboid buildings with open terraces facing the sea. The upper floors were mainly apartments, all with characteristic, blue-painted wooden balcony fences.

In the centre of the promenade, a little, rust-domed, whitewashed edifice, the church of Agios Nikolaos of Agera, stood proud, its bell always ready to call time on the line of restaurants on either side of it. Smaller, yet somehow demanding respect, it formed a focal point, dominating the seafront that faced the harbour.

The promenade was busy but not as bustling as it had been earlier in the day. There was still considerable activity in the bars and restaurants, with some people who'd come out for an early evening, and others who hadn't yet gone back to their hotels after their daytime adventures. However, one large contingent of the earlier crowd had gone. Most of the cruise passengers were already back on board, ready to sail in the early evening. The flotilla of sea taxis had slowed to a trickle, now serving hotel residents rather than cruise ship passengers.

It was still only about 19:00, well before the card game rendezvous.

"Good spot for a sundowner, Bernard?" suggested Justin.

"I think so, Justin," his friend agreed, "but let's try Little Venice. They say that's the best spot to watch the sunset."

The two men strolled along the harbour front, passing the fishing boat pier. Beyond the sea bus jetty, Bernard noted a series of exotic bars, one of which was advertising a drag show. A very camp waiter was mopping seats and tables, which had been sprayed by breaking waves at high tide.

"Maybe we can go and spend our winnings from the card game in there later, Justin?"

"You could enter the show, Bernard. You've got the curves."

"But not the clothes or the makeup!"

They laughed together, continuing a short distance to where Mykonos Castle, a partially restored monastery, overlooked a section of rocky shoreline. A number of people were gathered on the rocks beside the old monastery in prime positions to photograph the approaching sunset.

Just beyond the castle, they arrived at Little Venice, a famed alley with a terrace of buildings constructed immediately on the shoreline. Functioning as designer clothes shops, souvenir shops, cafes and cocktail bars, the businesses all had waterside rooms or terraces that overlooked the Aegean, in perfect positions for watching the sunset.

Bernard and Justin walked through a café to the outer terrace, which linked to several cocktail bars.

"The prices here are ridiculously high," noted Bernard, "but I guess it's worth it to watch the sunset."

"What sunset, Bernard? There's a little obstruction this evening!" Justin pointed out.

Looking outward, Bernard was shocked to see a twelve-deck cruise ship anchored about 600 metres away, directly in the path of the descending sun.

"Surely they can't park there?" muttered Bernard.

Just beyond the Little Venice bars was a 200-metre-long peninsula on which stood a row of six whitewashed windmills—the iconic image associated with Mykonos. Several dozen people were already gathered at the end of the peninsula, waiting for the perfect sunset.

"That'll do!" Justin exclaimed, pointing towards the windmills. "We can see past the cruise ship from there. Sod the cocktails."

For the next hour, they sat at the end of the peninsula, watching the sun drop behind Baos Island and Rhenia—a perfect, slow-motion colour change from yellow to orange, then to a grey and pink sky, unhampered by the cruise liner that blocked the view from Little Venice.

As the sun disappeared, dozens of people strolled around the windmills, many taking photographs and selfies against a stunningly coloured sky.

The two men returned to the harbour front in search of a bar. Finding a table from which they would have a good view across the port, they ordered beers and sat, mostly in silence, Bernard people-watching, Justin studying the seascape.

A short horn blast from the cruise ship moored at the New Port signalled its imminent departure. The two others, anchored in the bay, would follow suit within the hour, transporting their payloads slowly across the Aegean.

On the open upper decks, some passengers watched the buildings and features of Mykonos Town slowly merging into a greying blur as their ship sailed away from the island. In the interior lounges and restaurants, the travellers dined or enjoyed evening entertainment before retiring to their cabins for the night, anticipating a brief visit to another island tomorrow.

Justin watched with interest as a handful of fishing boats returned to the port to unload their catch. There seemed to be a larger number of boats preparing to go out for overnight fishing. They would probably return in the morning to supply a fresh 'catch of the day' to the many local seafood restaurants.

Meanwhile, Bernard studied the passing people, instinctively guessing who was gay and who wasn't. They slowly sipped their beers as twilight crept away and the sky began to darken.

"Time to go, Bern," said Justin. "It's nearly 8:30, and we still haven't eaten."

"Herm recommended the food at the Glorious Bar. If we go now, we should have time to order something before the card game," suggested Bernard.

They strolled around to the back of the nearby Agios Nikolaos of Agera church and into the network of narrow, Cycladic crazy-paved alleyways that linked the commercial area of the old town. Street and alleys of dark grey, random-shaped paving stones, their concrete rendering painted over by wide bands of white, cried out to be explored by curious visitors.

Within minutes, the alley they had chosen widened into a small, open square. Along one side, there were half a dozen brightly painted tables, some wooden, others of cast iron, each accompanied by several decorative, wrought iron chairs and cushioned benches. A few of the tables were occupied by couples sipping beer or cocktails. Attached to the underside of first-floor balconies, a large wreath of bougainvillea bushes flanked the area. Their bright pink flowers, now greying in the fading light, overhung some of the tables, providing a soft, scented backdrop.

Behind and between the tables, in the middle of a whitewashed wall, a dark green double door was thrown open on both sides, inviting curious passersby to enter. Above the door, illuminated by soft lighting on either side, was a sign declaring the open house to be ‘Glorious’.

A plaque on one side of the door gave the location title ‘Glorious’ with ‘Cocktail Bar and Meze Restaurant’ added as a subtitle. On the other side of the door, a blackboard was painted with a handwritten description of today’s menu items and drinks.

“I think we’ve found the venue,” declared Bernard confidently. “Should we sit out here or go inside?”

“We should go straight in. The minstrels will be here soon. If we’re playing cards, then I guess we need a big enough table on the inside before it starts getting busy.”

They ventured through the open doors, studying the interior as they walked slowly into the Glorious Bar. The lighting was soft but sufficient to provide a warm and welcoming ambience to an indoor space decorated in relatively cool, soothing colours. The interior was constructed like a cavern, with several wide arches stretching across the width from side to side. This gave the impression of a 10-

metre-wide tunnel between two streets, linking front and back entrances about 16 metres apart.

The walls and woodwork were painted primarily sage or olive green, with some partitions having a white-painted, natural stone facing. The walls were adorned by a number of art-nouveau paintings, reminiscent of attempts from a budding Picasso. About a third of the way through the tunnel, there was a four-metre-long bar with a solid, hardwood worktop along the righthand side of the tunnel. In front of the bar stood a row of half a dozen sage-painted wooden barstools. Opposite the bar and in some of the alcoves between the arches were groups of tables, chairs, and some well-cushioned sofas.

A pleasant aroma of fragrant herbs, spices, barbecued fish, and possibly some incense danced through the air, swinging to the sound of soft jazz-rock music. A few people were eating or drinking at some of the tables. To their amusement, a couple of very friendly cats were brushing against them, purring softly to the jazz as if singing for their supper.

"Not just Delos that's overrun by cats," said Justin. "Seems Mykonos has its own fair share."

A tabby with large white patches gently stroked itself against Bernard's ankles while he bent down to scratch behind its ears.

Turning towards the bar, Justin surveyed the shelves of spirits and wines, then noticed that a lady with long dark hair was smiling at him from the service area.

"Oh, hello," he said. "I didn't see you there."

"Kalispera, I'm Cristina," the lady replied with a smile. "Can I help you? Would you like to have a look at our menu?" she added, offering him the menu card.

"We're expecting some friends. I think we will be five people," said Bernard.

"Or maybe seven?" Cristina suggested knowingly. "We've had a reservation from Hermes for seven people from 9:00."

"That'll be them, I think," replied Justin. "There can't be too many Hermes around."

"It's their charade," smiled Cristina. "They all pretend to be Greek gods, but I think they're just a little cult group who want to create a new religion from an old one."

Justin laughed. "That sounds just like Hermes and co."

"I've reserved the alcove beside the other street entrance for you. They said they needed space for six people to play cards. But please be aware, there is to be no gambling. Playing games is OK, but we don't have a licence for gambling."

"No problem," replied Justin. "We'll just play for matchsticks or something. No money involved."

The two friends scanned the menu, agreeing on two Mythos beers, a Greek salad, hummus with pitta bread and a gyros platter to share. They then moved to the reserved alcove, where two four-person tables had been placed together to form six places. Against the adjacent wall was a lounge sofa with an ample supply of cushions. They sat down facing each other at one of the tables.

"You may have been saved by the house rules here, Bern," said Justin. "No gambling. So, your money is safe."

"Don't be boring, Justin. The gods will find a way. Don't forget; it's my lucky day!" Bernard laughed.

After a few minutes, the beers were served, followed ten minutes later by the spread of very tasty-looking food they had ordered.

"Oh dear, Justin. You're going to have to eat most of this, or I'll need a bigger pair of Speedos."

They spent the next fifteen minutes savouring the Greek dishes, but there was still plenty left when Hermes, Dionysus and Hephaestus arrived. The gods had changed from their beachwear (or lack of!) into bohemian clothing: brightly coloured open shirts exposing dangling medallions, with loose-fitting cotton trousers and leather sandals. Their appearance was more akin to travelling musicians than Greek gods.

Dionysus carried a gourd bottle dangling on a leather strap from his shoulder. An open shirt in multiple shades of red blended nicely with his eyes. Hermes sported shades of blue, and Hephaestus a gentler mix of greens and browns.

"Good evening, gentlemen," said Hermes with a friendly smile. "Ready to lose your money?"

"Ha, ha," Bernard laughed. "Not according to Paul, uh … I mean Apollo. He said this would be my lucky day."

"He'll be joining us shortly," said Hephaestus. "He's playing, too, so maybe he told you that just to persuade you to join the game?"

"Don't forget, Hephacstus, Apollo always tells the truth. He said it would be Bernard's lucky day, so it must be," Hermes reminded them.

"What if Apollo is really just a guy called Paul, acting out a Greek god charade?" added Justin. "Maybe you're all just actors playing a role here, in which case Bernard's predicted luck is also a fantasy."

The three gods looked at Justin, then at each other, and then back at Justin. Serious expressions, eye to eye. Who would blink first?

"How dare you doubt us, sir?" muttered Hermes, his amiable expression now becoming an angry one.

"Should I turn him into a rabbit?" asked Hephaestus. "Then he'll realise he should fear the gods."

"Or maybe just give him the Medusa look and turn him to stone," suggested Dionysus.

Bernard trembled a little. These guys really appeared to be serious. "Careful, Justin, we don't want to offend our friends here, do we?"

Justin laughed out loud. "Don't you see it, Bern? These guys are just as good actors as they are musicians. They're winding you up in advance of the card game, and then they'll take you to the cleaners. They'll bluff you to kingdom come!"

Hermes shot another serious glance at Justin, then grinned broadly and gave Bernard a hearty slap on the back, laughing loudly.

"I can see we're in for a fun evening, my friends," he said happily.

Even Dionysus managed a smile while Hephaestus winked at Justin as if to say, "You've called our bluff."

"Carry on with your meal, gentlemen," said Hermes. "There's no hurry."

"Plenty of food here, if any of you want to help us finish," replied Bernard, relaxing after a few concerned moments.

"Thank you, sir. It looks very good," Hephaestus said genuinely to Bernard before taking a slice of pitta bread, dipping it in the hummus, and following up with some pieces of pork gyros.

The three gods ordered a litre pitcher of red house wine, asking for seven glasses. Before it was served to the table, Apollo entered the bar, turning the heads of the various other customers who had come in as the evening progressed. A shirt as white as his perfect teeth hung open, allowing the laurel wreath medallion to catch the light as it swung against a dark, bronze chest.

Artemis followed close behind, wearing her crescent moon hair clasp and a characteristic camouflage fatigues outfit. Carrying a briefcase like a professional solicitor, she raised nearly as many eyebrows as Apollo.

"They're actors pretending to be Greek gods," Cristina whispered to the few people sitting on the bar stools.

"They certainly have the looks!" exclaimed one customer, glancing while trying not to stare as Apollo and

Artemis strolled into the alcove where the friends were gathered.

Dionysus carefully poured a liberal amount of red wine into each of the seven glasses before ordering another pitcher from the bar.

As they approached the table, Apollo looked Bernard directly in the eye.

"Good evening, Bernard," said Apollo, with an elegant grace and a disarming smile that nearly knocked Bernard off his seat.

"Hi, Paul, or would you prefer that I call you Apollo?" Bernard replied, convinced that his newfound friend was definitely gay.

"Well, now you know who we really are, it's probably best to call me Apollo," the god replied through gleaming white teeth that stretched across his bronzed jaws in a wide smile.

Justin guffawed loudly, "These guys really are convincing, Bernard. Prepare to be seriously bluffed out of your cash."

Artemis gave Justin a disdainful look. Dionysus reflected again on the benefits of turning him to stone, but recognised that that would cut a fun night short.

Hephaestus looked Dionysus in the eye knowingly. "That would be divine intervention," Hephaestus mouthed quietly to his friend. "Not permitted!"

Dionysus grinned and nodded in acknowledgement.

The two mortals finished the remains of their dinner with some assistance from Hephaestus and Dionysus.

"That was an excellent meal. Very well chosen," said Hephaestus to Bernard.

As Cristina brought the second carafe of wine, she reminded the group in the alcove, "Remember, no money on the table. We're not licensed for gambling."

"Of course not," said Hermes, beaming with his most honest assurance. "We only play for little pieces of plastic."

Relaxing on the cushioned sofa, Artemis smiled and instinctively patted her briefcase full of casino chips.

Cristina cleared away the food plates, leaving just the wine glasses on the table. As she walked away from the alcove, Hermes smiled around the table and asked Justin, "Do you know the rules of Texas Hold'em?"

"We can both play poker. If we play a few rounds with no stakes, then hopefully we can get the gist," replied Justin.

"OK then. Before we start, I'll explain quickly. The dealer deals two cards to each player. These are the 'Hole' cards. The player to the left of the dealer is the 'Small Blind'.

He must place half the minimum bet. In our game, that'll be one. The player to the left of the Small Blind is called the 'Big Blind'. He places double the Small Blind bet, so that's two, making an initial pot of three.

"Then, starting with the player to the left of the Big Blind, the players bet on their Hole cards. Each player must bet by 'Calling' or equalling the Big Blind bet, by 'Raising' it, or by "Folding'. Each player must equal the previous Call or Raise to stay in the game.

"After the 'Blind' round of betting, the dealer turns over three cards, known as the 'Flop'. Then there is a second round of betting, starting with the person immediately left of the dealer. This is based on the Hole cards plus the Flop cards. If you think you've got a strong hand, you can Call or Raise the bet in each betting round.

"The dealer then turns a fourth card, the 'Turn', and the players bet again.

"Finally, the Dealer turns a fifth card, called the 'River', and there is a final round of betting, at the end of which there is a Showdown between any players who haven't yet Folded their cards.

"The dealer role moves to the left with each round, so nobody should have an advantage, such as always being the Dealer or Big Blind.

Hermes glanced at Bernard and Justin in turn and added, "That may sound complicated, but if you know the ranking of poker hands, then you'll get used to the betting rules."

"I'm sure we can work it out, Hermes. Let's play two or three hands as a practice run," said Justin.

"Agreed, but first, we need some chips. Art, do you have the case?"

"I do," replied Artemis, bringing her briefcase to the table.

"Now, my friends," said Hermes, "we haven't discussed how much you can afford to lose to us, have we?"

"Or how much of your busking takings you're prepared to lose to us," interjected Bernard.

"Then I'll suggest a maximum personal stake of 500€. Is that acceptable to you?"

"That's a lot of money, Bernard. You could do a lot of night-clubbing for that," counselled Justin.

"At Mykonos prices? Anyway, we're going to be on the winning side, remember."

Artemis laid a green felt cloth marked for Texas Hold'em poker across the tables, then opened a wooden box containing stacks of poker chips.

"White is 1, Red is 5, Blue is 10, Green is 25, Black is 100. If we all start with 10 white, 8 red, 8 blue, 4 green and 1 black, then that comes to 330€ as a personal starting pot. If you lose it, you can buy in up to another 170€, but that's the limit. I don't want to completely ruin your holiday in Mykonos."

Artemis counted out the initial chip combination for each of the players. In turn, she held out her hand to Bernard and Justin and said, "330 euros, please."

Justin sighed deeply as they counted out the money for their chip purchase.

"Don't worry," said Hermes. "Artemis has our bank in her briefcase. We have the money to cash any chips you hold when we finish. We'll play three hands first so you can see how the betting works."

Hermes sat at the end of the table, with Bernard on his left and Justin on his right, facing each other. Apollo sat at the other end, facing Hermes, with Hephaestus between Justin and Apollo and Dionysus between Apollo and Bernard.

"I'll deal first," Hermes stated. "That makes Justin Small Blind and Hephaestus Big Blind for this hand."

Hermes dealt the players two cards each. Justin and Hephaestus put one white and two white chips onto the table, respectively, leaving Apollo to start the betting for the Blind round. All players happily put two white chips on the table, equal to the Big Blind bet, in the knowledge that no money would be lost on this hand.

Hermes then dealt the three-card Flop: king of spades, four of hearts and ace of hearts. The second round of betting started with Justin to the left of the dealer. With the five of clubs and eight of spades, Justin would have folded if money was being bet, but he decided to call, placing two chips on the table. Hephaestus, with the five and king of hearts, matched the call as he had four hearts, with two more cards to be played. With the three of diamonds and king of clubs, Apollo chose to fold. Dionysus, with the nine of hearts and ten of diamonds, also folded. Bernard matched the call as he had a pair of twos. Hermes, who had the ace of clubs and four of clubs, now had two pairs, aces high, since the Flop.

Hermes dealt the Turn card, they had another round of betting, followed by dealing of the River card, and a last round of betting. At the end of the game, Hermes' pairs of aces and fours were still the winning hand, so he took the pot.

At the end of the four rounds of betting, Bernard and Justin were both down about 30€. However, had they been playing for money, both may have folded earlier rather than risking poor hands.

After three games, they found themselves considering the cards that were dealt more carefully and tailoring their bets accordingly. They also started to pay attention to the expressions of the other players.

Who looked confident? Who sighed or grimaced when the cards were dealt? Did any of the gods exchange signals or expressions?

Bernard and Justin would have been losing between 40 and 50€ each after three games.

"Now it's time to play for real," said Hermes.

The chips were redistributed so that all players had their original 330€ pot. After the three practice games, the dealer role had moved around to Apollo. Dionysus and Bernard were now Small Blind and Big Blind, respectively. They initialised the pot with three white chips as before, and then betting on the Hole cards proceeded.

After another two games, Dionysus pointed out that the wine carafe was empty but elected to fill it from his gourd bottle.

"I've agreed a generous corkage fee with the bar manager," he stated as a very deep red liquid rose up the sides of the carafe. He then filled the glasses around the table with his 'special brew'.

"Special brew?" inquired Justin. "Are you trying to get us drunk?"

"Maybe it'll improve your confidence for taking a few risks," said Dionysus with a wry smile.

Justin took a sip from his glass. As he swilled it around his tongue, he felt an explosion of flavours. Sweet berries, honey, aromatic plants, and a lot of alcohol stunned his taste buds into submission to something he had never before experienced.

"Whoa! This is nectar!" he exclaimed

"How does he know that?" asked Hephaestus, looking at Dionysus. "Has he had it before?"

"The mortals use 'nectar' as a figure of speech for a very nice drink," Apollo replied. "Few have experienced the real thing."

Observing his friend's reaction to Dionysus's brew, Bernard sipped from his glass.

His eyes rolled, and he was speechless for a good half minute before exclaiming, "Oh my! This is something else! Is it some sort of absinthe? It's certainly a very powerful potion! Is this hallucinogenic? Are you trying to get us drunk?"

"Everybody around the table is sharing this very special brew that Dionysus has prepared from fine natural ingredients in Naxos. If it's hallucinogenic, then we will all be hallucinating soon," Hermes replied, laughing.

During the next three hours, the poker game continued. The personal pots went up and down. Justin was convinced that the gods all knew what Hole cards each player held. They seemed to be betting to prolong the game, rather than to win quickly. Both Bernard and Justin won a few hands with pots that had been raised. Both had doubled their money and their confidence at some point in the evening. They were beginning to believe they would leave the bar significantly better off.

Justin did find it strange that Dionysus appeared to fill the carafe several times from his gourd, even though the carafe was larger! He also noted that when Dionysus was dealing, he always received two twos of different suits. He stopped short of openly calling Dionysus a cheat.

As the night progressed, luck swung like a pendulum, but gradually seemed to gravitate to Apollo and Hermes. Justin and Bernard watched their stack of chips shrink until there were none left. Bernard opted to purchase another 170€ worth, but Justin was sensible enough to cut his loss at 330€ and drop out of the game. Dionysus was next to drop out, sipping his brew as his eyes got redder.

During the last game, Bernard had been dealt the seven and eight of spades, Hermes, the king of diamonds and ace of clubs, and Apollo, the five of spades and six of diamonds. Since both Hermes and Bernard were looking confident and quick to call on the blind bet, Apollo chose to fold and leave the game.

The Flop revealed the four of diamonds, king of spades and ace of spades. Bernard now had four spades, but Hermes had a pair of kings and a pair of aces. The bets were raised and called.

The Turn revealed the two of spades. Bernard decided to go all in, placing all of his remaining chips, about 100€, in the pot. Hermes looked at Bernard.

"You look nervous. I think you're bluffing," said Hermes.

"Or maybe you are?" Bernard responded.

Hermes matched Bernard's all-in bet.

The River revealed the six of spades. Bernard already had a spades flush. Hermes had a pair of kings and a pair of aces.

"Flush beats two pairs," Bernard beamed, having at least won some of his initial stake back.

Bernard and Justin were now very wobbly after consuming much too much of Dionysus's brew.

It's no wonder he always has red eyes, thought Justin.

Bernard turned to Apollo.

"You said I was going to win somebody's ass tonight," he slurred, confident after the last victory. Bernard had been hoping that he had a secret tryst with Apollo, who might now respond.

"You've only played for money. Not for anybody's ass," Apollo replied.

"How about yours then?" Bernard smiled suggestively.

"I'm not that way inclined, darling," Apollo replied teasingly.

Disappointed, Bernard turned to Hermes.

"You're the expert card player here, Herm. How about the rest of my chips against your ass?"

"That's not a poker game bet. Why don't we just cut the cards?" suggested Hermes.

"Fine by me," slurred Bernard.

Hermes picked up and shuffled the card deck, then placed it neatly on the table.

"You cut first, Bernard."

Bernard reached toward the pack and picked a small block of cards from the top, then turned over the card below. Six of hearts! Bernard's chin fell a little. Was his stupidity going to cost him his winnings? Justin tutted at him in disgust.

Hermes picked another group of cards off the pack, turning the next card face up. Four of clubs.

"Yes!" exclaimed Bernard, clenching his fists and grinning. "Apollo always tells the truth! I've won your ass!"

"What do you want with my ass anyway?" asked Hermes.

"I wanna roger that pretty ass of yours!"

Justin put his elbows on the table and dropped his head into his hands. Why was his friend such an idiot?

"Roger my ass?" replied Hermes, frowning and looking very concerned. "I need a few minutes to compose myself. I'm just going outside. Give me three minutes, then follow me out."

"No running away now," said Bernard.

"A bet is a bet. Three minutes," replied Hermes.

The group watched in bewilderment as Hermes walked quickly to the door and disappeared into the street outside.

Bernard watched the second hand of his watch tick away very slowly. At the end of the three minutes, he stood up, winked at Justin, smiled and said, "See you later."

Justin and the gods looked at each other in mild embarrassment. Artemis frowned in disgust at the behaviour of mortals before remembering the activities to which her own father was prone.

Suddenly, they all raised their heads in unison as a loud yell came from the street.

"You bastard! You bastard!" Bernard was shouting.

They all ran through the door and looked in the direction in which Bernard was yelling. A set of yellowing teeth was smiling at him from a hairy face, wearing a wide-brimmed straw hat through which a pair of long pointed ears had been pushed. A neckband clearly marked with the name "Roger" swung beneath the donkey's chin as it looked back at Bernard and gave him a loud "Eeeyaaww".

The person who had tied Roger the ass to the railing next door to the Glorious laughed loudly from the end of an alleyway a few metres behind Roger. Bernard ran towards Hermes, ready to punch him in the face if he could catch him. Hermes disappeared around the corner. Bernard arrived at the corner seconds later, but Hermes was nowhere to be seen.

Where is he? How did he move so quickly? thought Bernard as he turned to walk back to Justin and the other gods.

All of them were in stitches. Bernard had never seen Justin laugh so much. Justin and Dionysus were so amused that they were even hugging each other.

"Bloody good stuff you've brewed there, Dionysus. Let me have the name so I can buy some in the supermarket," Justin fruitlessly requested.

Bernard turned to Apollo. "I suppose you think that was funny?" he blurted.

"I guess it must have been. Everybody is laughing a lot," replied Apollo.

"At my expense!" exclaimed Bernard angrily.

"Well, with relation to expense, why don't you check Roger's saddlebag?"

Bernard looked towards the donkey. It did have a saddlebag hanging on its back. Opening it, Bernard was surprised to find a roll of euro notes with a handwritten scrap of paper attached. "1000€ to Bernard and Justin for entertainment value. Enjoy the rest of your holiday, H."

Justin was still tittering as he approached Bernard. "Maybe they weren't such bad con men after all, Bern. I take back everything I said."

The two friends looked at the group of gods and the goddess with whom they'd spent the evening. All smiled amicably. A few hands were shaken, and farewells exchanged before Bernard and Justin staggered off back to their hotel, having made a significant profit during the strangest card game they'd ever played.

Chapter 10: Goddesses on Naxos Beach

In the guest room at the Ambrosia Taverna in Naxos, Athena stirred after a sound sleep. Even a goddess could be stressed by the events of the past few days. Her irritation with the tourists in Athens, followed by extensive travelling and then attempting to persuade the other gods to agree with her opinions, had exhausted her. At the start of a new day, she felt relaxed and ready to shut out the problems that had led her to her current quest. A day on the beach would be a welcome break.

She dressed in swimwear, covered by a beach wrap, and headed down to the terrace where she had enjoyed the company of Hestia, Demeter and Persephone the previous evening. At the back of the terrace, a breakfast buffet had already been prepared. The smell of freshly baked bread and brewing coffee offered something as delicious as nectar.

Scanning the terrace, she spotted her fellow goddesses sharing a table in the morning sunshine. The table had been laid for four. There was a cushioned chair waiting for her.

"Athena, my dear," Hestia greeted her. "Let me pour you some coffee and orange juice. Help yourself to the buffet."

Athena took her seat at the table.

"I'm sorry if you've been waiting for me. Have you been here long? I'll grab some food in a few minutes," she said to Demeter and Persephone.

"Not at all, Athena. We served the mortal residents their breakfast first. Now we can sit down and enjoy ours at our leisure. Did you sleep well? You must have been very tired," said Demeter.

"I had a wonderful sleep. I feel like I'm on holiday," replied Athena.

A few of the taverna's resident tourists were still having their breakfast at a handful of the dining tables, but there was still a wide choice of food options on the buffet. Yoghurt and dried fruit, cereals, fresh bread, cold meats, cheeses, cakes and homemade biscuits. Bacon and eggs in heated containers, some salad options, and fresh fruit. The residents could finish breakfast without assistance from their hosts.

Athena rose again and walked to the buffet, where she selected several items before returning to the table.

"The breakfast spread is perfect," she observed.

Hestia placed a glass of freshly squeezed orange juice and a cup of coffee in front of Athena.

"There's milk in the jug there on the table if you need it, my dear," she said with a warm smile.

"You're so welcoming. Thank you, all."

Athena felt a pang of jealousy. Her fellow immortals were almost living the life of mortals but in a beautiful setting by the beach. Here, there were no crowds, just the sound of the waves washing onto the sand. The sweet scents of flowers and aromatic plants mingled with the aromas from Demeter's kitchen.

Hestia and Demeter busied themselves, ensuring the remaining taverna guests had everything they needed and then clearing tables as they were vacated. They left Athena and Persephone to share their breakfast time together.

"I love it here," said Athena, turning to Persephone. "I can see why you come back here every spring, Persephone. It must be a complete contrast with the underworld."

"It certainly is, Athena," Persephone replied. "It's paradise. The warmth of the sun, the sweet sounds and smells of the beach and the flowers. It's beautiful."

"But you're serving mortals. How can that be right?"

"Mother and Hestia explained all that. It's who they are. They are the essence of hospitality and good food. They are simply continuing their divine roles. That's why they don't see a need to join you in pursuing the things you wish for."

"And you? Your immortal role is not here in Naxos."

"No, I'm the queen of the dead half of the time. I can help serve the living during the other half," replied Persephone. "This is a bit of a heavy conversation. Why don't we enjoy our breakfast for a while, then we can go to the beach. We'll have lots of time to discuss serious matters later."

"You're right, Persephone. I do too much thinking sometimes," Athena replied.

The two goddesses laughed together, then lightened the conversation while they continued their breakfast.

By the time Athena and Persephone had finished eating, all of the other tables had been vacated. They helped Hestia and Demeter clear away the buffet and clean the dining area after breakfast.

"All done here now, Athena," said Persephone. "Time to head to the beach if you like?"

"Yes, lovely idea, Persephone. I had a brief visit to the beach in Cyprus with Aphrodite, but it wasn't peaceful like here. It will be nice to just lie in the sun or swim in the sea."

They collected towels and straw beach mats, then strolled the short distance to a quiet section of beach among the coves by the cedar grove. Choosing a flat section of sand, sheltered from the breeze by a granite outcrop, they laid the mats and towels out for themselves to relax on.

Athena sat on her towel, looking across the sea to Paros in the distance. Although there were a few mortals scattered around the beach, their cove was secluded and private.

"This is very peaceful, Persephone. I can understand why you like to come here."

"Yes, it's a complete contrast to the underworld. Hades doesn't know what he's missing."

"Haven't you tried to persuade him to come to Naxos? It might cheer him up after all that time in the darkness of his kingdom."

"He's the king of the dead! He's not supposed to be cheerful!" Persephone exclaimed with a rueful smile.

"Do you think he'll join us in Athens?" Athena asked Persephone.

"Definitely not!" Persephone responded emphatically.

"Why are you so sure, Persephone?"

"Think about it, Athena," she replied. "Why would it matter to him? The only time he's ever come to the Earth's surface was to kidnap me. It was all over in seconds. I was picking flowers, and the Earth split open in a huge crevasse. He emerged and grabbed me onto his chariot. Then he turned the chariot back into the crevasse, and it closed behind us.

"He has never interacted with living mortals and has no need to. There are no temples in honour of Hades. Nobody in their right mind prays to him, except maybe to ask for a dead relative to be released back to life. That's never going to happen. Nobody makes sacrifices to him. In fact, everybody wants to avoid him, and they are all scared of ever meeting him.

"Ironically, they will all meet him in the end. The Fates will decide when. Hades doesn't kill people. Life does! The one certainty about mortal life is that it will end, and every lost soul will go to the underworld."

"Provided they've paid the ferryman," noted Athena.

"Of course. Charon must be paid to ferry them across the River Styx at the end of the world. Otherwise, they remain as ghosts: those lost souls who can't get into the underworld."

"So, you're saying Hades won't be sympathetic to my cause?" asked Athena.

"He isn't particularly sympathetic to anybody, Athena. He rules the kingdom of the dead. He loves me dearly, and that is his one concession to emotions. Hades will not want to party in Athens. Especially with his two brothers! He dislikes Poseidon and is jealous of Zeus for being king of the gods. He will not want to see either of them."

"Can I remind you that I'm not organising a party, Persephone," said Athena. "This is a serious matter about the future of the Olympians."

"I get that, Athena, but you need to lighten up. If you get Hermes, Hephaestus and Dionysus together, there will be a party whether you like it or not. You can try to set the guidelines, but I think they'll all be more sympathetic with you if you stand back a little and let them play."

"Play! They're supposed to be gods. They should be above playing!" declared Athena.

"Maybe you need to spend six months a year in the underworld, Athena. I am queen down there, with the austere god who I have come to love. I can tell you it's no party. When I come to Naxos each year to join my mother and Hestia, life is renewed. We party in our own way. We are happy. Life is fun. You should try it," suggested Persephone.

Athena reflected on Persephone's message. Maybe she did take everything a bit too seriously.

"I can see how you would enjoy coming back to Naxos every springtime. But you return to your husband in the autumn again. Is that not also something that makes you happy?"

"Yes, of course," said Persephone, "but it's six months of closeness with a lover in an otherwise dark place. It's a combination of desire and duty. My real happiness comes when returning to the light, even without my lover."

"It's hard for me to imagine how that feels. Athens is my love. I am there all the time, but I see it declining from its former glory. I feel angry when I witness that happening. I want to intervene to restore its greatness. But I don't feel love for any partner."

"You have chosen to live as a virgin," replied Persephone. "Like Hestia and Artemis, you are free to make all your own decisions. Your existence is not tied up with that of another. You are free. But maybe that means sacrificing the closeness you could have had in a strong relationship with another."

"Hestia has the companionship of Demeter and, of course, of yourself six months of the year."

"And Dionysus, too!" added Persephone. "He may travel with his fellow gods, but his home is here on Naxos. He met his wife, Ariadne, here after she had been dumped by Theseus. She helped Theseus kill the Minotaur and showed him how to escape from the labyrinth in Knossos, yet he still dumped her! How mean is that?"

"I heard that Dionysus saw Theseus and Ariadne asleep and was so attracted to her that he told Theseus to leave her on Naxos and return to Athens alone. Is this not so?"

"It was written in the stars, Athena, or at least in the myths," said Persephone with a smile.

"Naxos is an important place for the Olympians then, it seems," noted Athena.

"Yes, of course. The home of Hestia, Demeter, Dionysus, and myself part of the time. Also, Poseidon stole his wife Amphitrite from here before taking her to the depths of the sea. There are temples here to Apollo, Demeter and Dionysus. The Temple of Demeter is older than the Parthenon in Athens. People worshipped the fertility goddess there even before they knew about the other Olympians. The highest mountain here is Mount Zas, which the locals claim is where Zeus was raised."

"But he was raised on Crete," Athena observed.

"It's good for Naxian tourism for them to claim him as one of theirs," replied Persephone with a knowing smile.

"I always thought Athens was the most important place for the Olympians, or maybe Mount Olympus."

"It's all partly due to the proximity of Delos. When Delos was the commercial centre of the Aegean, Naxos was a much larger and more fertile island nearby. It supplied food and building materials to Delos, the birthplace of Apollo and Artemis. The ancient peoples of the Cyclades islands made Delos a special place, with temples to Apollo and Artemis. Delos is now diminished to an uninhabited archaeological site, but Naxos always supported a bigger population and remains bustling and beautiful."

"Yes, I must say, Persephone," said Athena, "this is a beautiful island. All these long sandy beaches, with mountains and valleys behind. I'm sure Artemis would love it here too."

"Of course. The twins are also close to the other gods here on Naxos. We may be Olympians, but our hearts are in Naxos," Persephone replied before changing the topic. "Have you tried to ask Poseidon about going to Athens?"

"I know there's no point, Persephone," said Athena. "He bears a grudge. He wanted to be the god of Athens, but I was chosen instead, and he's shaken the Earth and churned up the sea ever since. Can you imagine if Poseidon had been the patron god of Athens instead of me? The city would have been controlled by seafarers and pirates instead of being the birthplace of justice, ethics and democracy."

"Call me Perse, Athena. Everyone else here does, and it's easier than Persephone," she said, feeling a growing warmth between the two half-sisters.

"Of course, Perse," replied Athena. "I think Poseidon will just keep his distance, but he'll try to cause me problems like he did for Odysseus when I was trying to help him get back to Ithaca after the Trojan War. Do you know it took him ten years to get home?"

"Yes, I've heard the stories of that journey. Poseidon can be very mean. Did you know that he raped my mother, his sister Demeter?"

"Really? That's horrible, but then that seems to be the nature of the senior male gods. Zeus is father to many mortals and immortals alike, ourselves included," said Athena.

"My mother was in mourning, trying to find me after I was kidnapped by Hades, but Poseidon pursued her. She turned herself into a mare to try to escape, but he transformed into a stallion and seduced her. I have a half-brother, Arion, who is a horse! He has a long face, just like Hades!"

The goddesses laughed loudly together at Persephone joking at her husband's expense.

"Poseidon has a thing about horses," Persephone continued. "It's said he created the first horse. When I sit here on the beach, I sometimes see him out at sea. He rides a chariot pulled by four white horses. They will sometimes appear at the surface in the distance before dropping deep below the waves again."

Athena and Persephone scanned the five-mile gap between their beach and Paros. The sea was mostly calm, but occasionally, a turbulently breaking stretch of white froth would appear on the surface before dispersing as quickly as it had appeared.

"Sometimes it's just waves breaking on the surface, but sometimes it's him. Riding his chariot with his trident poised, ready to whip up a storm," Persephone assured.

"Do you think he might try to communicate with us, Perse?"

"He'll know we're here. When we swim, there'll be hundreds of little eyes watching us—all those fish and sea creatures. He's watching us right now, but Poseidon doesn't communicate. He doesn't need to. He controls the mysterious deep blue sea. Mortals and immortals alike need to fear and respect him. There's a strange but reluctant connection between the depths of the sea and the underworld. Poseidon is almost as reclusive as Hades. Both are jealous of Zeus and of each other, so I don't think there's much point in asking him. He won't come to the party."

"It's not a party!" shouted Athena.

"It *is* a party!" replied Persephone, adding, "Dionysus will make sure of that!"

The two goddesses laughed loudly together and hugged tightly.

"OK, Perse. You've convinced me. I'll try not to be too serious, and hopefully, they'll all listen to me in Athens before painting the town red."

In the distance, a white vessel with dark blue waves painted on the side was approaching from the south. A large plume of white froth trailed behind it like a horizontal waterfall.

"That's the Seajet we'll be taking tomorrow," said Persephone. "It's just come from Santorini and Ios. It'll be carrying over a thousand island hoppers at about 40 knots."

They watched the progress of the fast ferry as it approached them, then rounded a headland towards Naxos Town.

"It'll make a nice change from flying," said Athena with a smile.

The two goddesses talked at length about Athens, Naxos, Greece, the Olympians, the tourists, life, death and immortality. Occasionally, they swam together, following fish and searching for shells on the bottom of the sea, and then rested on the beach again. They had known of each other for thousands of years but had never had cause to speak at length. Now, they found themselves enjoying a newfound companionship.

"Maybe I should go up to Athens from time to time. It will always be fun to catch up with each other," said Persephone.

"Or I should sometimes come to Naxos. I'll probably let my hair down a bit more than I would in Athens. I can relax here without frowning at the crowds by the Parthenon."

"It's a deal, Athena. Closer friends from now on. When you live for thousands of years, you need some variety in your life."

Both laughed again and went back to the taverna to drink to their renewed acquaintance and future friendship.

Chapter 11: Islands in the Wake of Poseidon

The morning after their day on the beach, Persephone and Athena enjoyed breakfast with Hestia and Demeter, then used the local bus service to travel to Naxos port. They arrived with an hour to spare before the departure of the Seajet to Mykonos and Piraeus. Leaving the bus at the shore end of the ferry pier, they chose a table at a nearby café and ordered some drinks.

A narrow promenade stretched 200m from the café to a small island, on which a series of steps rose to the remains of an archaic temple, dominated by an eight-metre-high square archway facing towards Delos. A breakwater stretched from the island westwards, protecting the approach to the harbour.

"That's the temple of Apollo," explained Persephone. "The archway is the Portara: the Great Doorway. It points towards Delos because that's the birthplace of Apollo. The Portara is made from four huge marble beams, which were put in place more than 2500 years ago. Before the Parthenon was built!"

"And now in ruins, just like the Parthenon," added Athena.

From their table, they looked along a causeway that connected the port to the island and its temple. The sea was considerably rougher than it had been the previous day. Large waves were breaking over the causeway and the breakwater. A dozen teenagers played cat and mouse with the breakers, unsuccessfully dodging the waves as they swamped the route to Apollo's temple. At least a dozen more people could be seen walking up the stepped pathway towards the temple, undoubtedly already soaked from running the gauntlet across the causeway.

A car ferry bound for Santorini sailed across open water towards the shelter of the harbour, rocking its way through the swell. Within about fifteen minutes, the ferry had entered the harbour, turned 180 degrees, emptied several hundred passengers, a few dozen cars and several lorries, reloaded with another swarm of passengers and cars, and departed back into the rough sea.

After finishing their coffees, Athena and Persephone walked down the pier to a covered waiting area near the ferry embarkation point, where they joined a crowd of more than one hundred other prospective passengers. Shortly before their scheduled departure, they could hear the loud rumbling of the Seajet engine as it passed well clear of the headland on the western tip of the island and turned south towards the shelter of Naxos port. It was a large catamaran, nearly 90 metres long, driven by rear water jets and capable of carrying 1100 passengers and 200 cars at 40 knots.

Just as the earlier ferry had done, the Seajet turned 180 degrees on approach to the pier, lowering embarkation ramps as it came closer. Within seconds of the ramps being set on the dockside, the waiting crowd were instructed to board while the disembarking passengers were crossing the dock in the opposite direction. Two mobs strode rapidly in contrasting directions, most pulling suitcases on wheels, trying to avoid each other as they mingled. Concurrently, one group of cars drove off the portside ramp while a new set of cars drove onto the starboard ramp.

"This is organised chaos," said Athena.

"Yes, it's amazing nobody gets trampled in the rush, but they all seem to get off or on as desired," Persephone replied as the two goddesses made their way to the ramp and onto the Seajet.

"It can't be easy for anybody who's elderly or infirm," Athena observed.

On board, most people were depositing suitcases on luggage racks on the lower car deck and then joining queues on staircases at either side of the boat. At the top of each staircase, crew members were scanning boarding passes. While standing in the queue on the stairs, Athena noted that the vessel was already moving out to sea and had begun rolling significantly with the swell.

After having their passes scanned, Athena and Persephone joined the large number of passengers staggering through the seating areas and searching for their pre-reserved seats. There were two seating decks, with seats organised into ranks to aid the numbering system. The two goddesses were fortunate to have seats by the window on the lower of the two decks, avoiding the need to climb another set of stairs on the rolling boat. The seats were large, reclined loungers. Once sat down, the rolling motion of the Seajet seemed less severe.

"This is more comfortable than I was expecting," Athena observed.

"It's a bit rough today, but it can get much worse," replied Persephone.

As the Seajet sailed out into the open water to the north of the harbour, the swell became noticeably more pronounced, but not a cause for concern. A crew member pointed out seasickness bags for those who needed them, but most passengers read books, slept or chatted, unperturbed by the rolling of the ship.

The windows were partly obscured by the spray thrown up as the bow slapped headlong into the waves, driven by a strong, northerly wind. Looking through the window, Persephone could see dark, blue-grey waves topped by white froth where the crests were broken by the wind.

"He's out there today, Athena," she declared. "I won't be surprised if he makes the journey a bit uncomfortable.

A large crowd waited on the quayside in front of the Harbour Authority buildings at the Mykonos New Port. The harbour area was a hive of activity: significantly busier than Naxos. In the past hour, two car ferries had arrived, emptied, reloaded and sailed off again.

A large cruise ship now occupied half the dock space. Cruise passengers continually streamed off, joining pre-organised groups taking coaches or being led to the sea bus and sea taxi services. Cars and foot passengers alike queued to join whichever vessel they were taking, while taxis and buses helped to hoover up the swarms of people waiting to travel into Mykonos Town or to other parts of the island.

Among the crowds waiting for the Seajet to Piraeus was an athletic lady with short dark hair wearing a camouflage-patterned outfit, her tall, blond, male-model-like brother, and three travellers in bohemian dress. The male model looked pensive.

"I foresee a three-fingered hand creating rocking and rolling," declared Apollo.

"Rocking and rolling?" Hermes questioned. "It's party time!"

"Just rock and roll? No sex and drugs?" Hephaestus sounded disappointed.

"I can supply some substances," Dionysus added. "Maybe Aphrodite can arrange some other pleasures?"

"Careful what you say, Dionysos. That's my wife you're talking about!" replied Hephaestus.

"Try telling Ares that," Dionysus replied.

"Stop the nonsense, boys," Artemis said with authority. "Apollo's Oracle never lies. The three-fingered hand is Poseidon's trident, and it's the sea that he's going to cause to rock and roll. Have you seen how rough the sea is? He knows we're travelling on it, and he's already playing his games."

"Don't burst our bubble, Artemis," demanded Hermes. "Even if Poseidon rocks the boat, we can still have a party when we get off at the other end."

As they waited on the dockside, the Seajet emerged into view, travelling north from the channel between Delos and Mykonos. Once it was well past the islands of Kavouras and

Baos, it turned east for the final stretch into Mykonos New Port, taking several large waves side on as it did so. The catamaran listed significantly, causing the prow to crash heavily into wave troughs as it turned. On board, several passengers gasped or let out cries as they were carried sideways, then dropped onto the sea, causing the whole vessel to shudder and drinks in plastic cups to fall from several tables.

"Here comes our boat," observed Hermes. "It's certainly rockin' and rollin'."

The sea was calmer closer to the harbour, allowing the Seajet to complete its 180-degree reversal into the dock while lowering its car and passenger ramps ready for a rapid turnaround.

Foot passengers, motorbikes and cars flooded across the ramps as the new load of passengers passed them to invade the seats that had just been emptied. Within ten minutes, the Seajet was on its way once more while passengers scrambled to find their reserved seats. Next stop, Syros, en route to Piraeus.

The five seats reserved by Artemis were just a few rows behind Persephone and Athena on the righthand side of the lower passenger deck. Artemis quickly occupied the window seat.

Hermes briefly moved to where Athena and Persephone were sitting and agreed with them that they should remain in their allotted seats rather than move around the boat in the rough seas. After the first 40 minutes, they would have a short stop at Syros.

Accelerating away from the harbour, blasting a large plume of white froth behind it, the Seajet headed westwards, moving out into the rougher waters of the open sea. Once past Baos and Kavouras, the route headed westwards past the north of Rhenia.

Persephone peered at the wave crests travelling to the southwest through the gap between Tinos and Mykonos, noting that the swaying of the boat was increasing.

"These waves are hitting us almost side on," she said to Athena.

"Have you seen him out there, Perse?" asked Athena.

"I'm looking for the white horses, but all I've seen so far is white spray where the wind catches the wave tops."

Artemis was also peering out at the sea. Large waves appeared to come towards the boat, almost straight into the side of the hull. Walls of dark grey water threatened to swamp them until the side of the boat rode up and over, slapping down at the bow, sending plumes of spray along the side of the vessel. As the boat rose up on one high wave, something caught her eye. The brow of a wave that was heading sideways towards them seemed to be topped by a long river of white. As she watched the wave, the white froth to her left, beyond the prow of the boat, became more clearly defined. It was difficult to focus through the spray covering the windows, but Artemis was sure she could pick out the shapes of four horses riding the crest of the wave, trailing white water behind them.

Then Persephone saw it, too. "Look," she said quietly, pulling Athena's arm towards her. "Outside the window. A long white crest."

Athena leaned over the top of Persephone. "I see it," she said. "I see him!"

Looking forward along the crest, Athena was sure she could see the form of a man among a group of horses. He had long, flowing white locks, blowing in the wind among the horse's manes, and he held something golden, pointing it forward.

As Athena peered towards the white mass, through the haze of spray, the prow of the Seajet veered to the right, crossing the wave diagonally. The bow lifted, and the starboard side of the boat rode up onto the crest, seemingly riding the wave like a surfboard, before sliding rapidly into the following trough. The double hull of the boat hit the bottom of the wave with a shudder that sent drink cups flying, startling crew members and passengers alike. Some passengers screamed. Somewhere among them, a baby began crying loudly. A small dog joined the chorus with a high-pitched yelp, answered by the deep bark of a large dog.

"What the hell was that?" yelled a nearby passenger. "A tsunami?"

"Not a tsunami. You don't notice those in deep water," a crew member assured. "Just a freak storm wave. We've had some very strong winds for the Aegean the last few days, especially in the north part. This has churned up the water."

Persephone and Athena glanced at each other knowingly.

"That was the wake of Poseidon," said Persephone confidently.

"I agree," replied Athena. "I saw him. He was riding his chariot, pulled by four horses. I saw his trident. That white crest was the wake that trailed behind him."

After the shock of the freak wave, the swell was less noticeable as the boat continued into the harbour at Syros. The gods took the opportunity of the short stop to leave their seats and reflect on the experience.

"It was Poseidon. I saw him riding the front of the wave crest," Artemis informed the group.

"Me too," added Persephone.

"And me," Athena confirmed. "He was holding out his trident and riding a chariot pulled by four horses."

"The three-fingered hand!" noted Apollo.

"Rock and roll!" stated Hermes.

"But why just rattle us like that? He could have sunk the boat if he'd wanted to," Hephaestus noted.

"That would be pointless," said Persephone. "We're immortal, so we would all have escaped anyway. If he'd sunk the boat, then he'd have killed the mortals on board."

"Would that have bothered him?" asked Dionysus.

"Probably not," said Athena, "but it's the Fates who decide when it's time for people to die. If it wasn't time for these people, then Poseidon could not kill them."

"Why would he want to kill either them or us?" asked Artemis. "He saved my mother Leto, allowing myself and Apollo to be born. He washed her boat up on the little floating island of Delos when Hera had forbidden her to land anywhere to give birth. Without the help of Poseidon, we wouldn't be here."

"We still have to get from Syros to Piraeus," Dionysos pointed out. "Maybe he's not finished with us yet."

"No, I think he just wanted to remind me that he still controls the sea," said Athena. "He wanted Athens too, so he's just reminding me he hasn't forgiven me for being the goddess of Athens."

"Yes, Poseidon is very like Hades. They're strong individuals, not part of Athena's team," added Persephone. "Like the underworld, the deep blue sea, the winds which stir it up, and the trembling of the Earth are dark, mysterious forces. Poseidon doesn't want us to forget that he is the power who controls the depths."

"Just like my mother on the island of Delos, we were just a tiny island in the wake of Poseidon. He had the power to destroy us if he'd wanted to," said Artemis.

While the Seajet prepared to leave Syros, the next batch of new passengers were arriving and seeking their seats. The Olympians returned to theirs, braced for Poseidon's impacts on the next leg of the journey. The boat pulled away from the harbour and then accelerated to its fast, cruising speed once it was well clear of the Syros shoreline. As they headed north, along the east coast of Syros, the boat continued to roll in the heavy swell but without any more hard impacts.

Once the boat had rounded the northern tip of Syros and turned west, the swell lessened, and the passengers could relax in comfort. Perhaps Poseidon had rocked the boat enough to satisfy his megalomania. Or, maybe they were travelling with the waves in a region of sea partly sheltered by the islands of Syros, Tinos and Andros. Whatever the reason, they had a smooth ride for the next two hours. They passed through the gulf between Kithnos and Kea, then sailed on calmer seas, eventually arriving on schedule at the Athenian port of Piraeus.

Spilling out of the car dock, along with hundreds of mortals, the gods and goddesses made their way quickly to the Piraeus metro station and boarded a Line 1 train. Leaving the train at Monastiraki station, they walked from Monastiraki Square, through streets thronging with tourists, to a path that climbed past the ancient Agora archaeological sites in the direction of the Acropolis.

As they neared the Acropolis, they heard excited voices.

"Did you see them?" a tourist was asking a group nearby.

"I saw them," replied a lady waving her mobile phone. "I have some pictures. Wanna see?"

"Oh, yes, please…Ooh, I can see them heading towards the trees!"

"Lots of people saw them, but nobody knows where they went," said the lady with the phone photos.

"The strange thing is, nobody saw them again after they landed," observed her husband. "They were definitely golden eagles. Strange to see them in the middle of Athens!"

"There was a couple who came out of the woods, who said they saw them up a tree, but they seem to have disappeared," said another person.

"Over there! That's the couple who were in among the trees!" noted another person, pointing to two people who were heading towards the path to Areopagus Hill.

"I think we've found Zeus and Hera," said Athena with a smirk.

Looking as godlike as Apollo and as bohemian as the minstrels, Zeus was smiling in their direction as he approached. He was accompanied by Hera in a flowing purple dress with a large peacock motif on the front. As the king and queen joined the group, the seven gods and goddesses all hugged each other in greeting.

"Have you seen Ares or Aphrodite?" asked Athena.

"Not yet," replied Zeus. "They'll arrive at least five minutes apart so that we'll all think they haven't just spent the night together in Athens."

Hera reddened. "How can you say that about our dear boy?" she snapped at Zeus.

"Well, what about our other dear boy, Hephaestus?" Zeus replied

Hermes thought it was time to change the subject. "OK, gang," laughed Hermes. "To Areopagus Hill."

The group followed along the path to Areopagus Hill, where they found a flat marble platform on which they could sit and view the surrounding city and its archaeological sites.

As Zeus predicted, Ares arrived ten minutes behind them and hugged each of his fellow Olympians in turn.

Aphrodite arrived ten minutes later, hugging each of the group and finishing with Ares.

"Hi, Ares," she smiled. "Haven't seen you for a long time."

Apollo, Hermes, Dionysus and Hephaestus all burst into fits of laughter.

Chapter 12: On Areopagus Hill

Tara, Chloe and Daphne took in the changing vistas as they climbed a winding path, passing the ancient Agora, towards a rocky outcrop just 150 metres west of the Acropolis entrance. They had driven back from the Olympus region early the previous day in their hire car to have time to visit some of the famous archaeological sites of Athens before flying home. The temperature in the mid-twenties was still well below the summer highs that would make a visit to Athens too unbearably tiring to be enjoyable.

After returning the car to the airport yesterday morning, they took the metro to Monastiraki Square and checked into a small hotel nearby. They spent the afternoon queuing and shuffling through the crowds at the Acropolis before exploring the tourist shops and finding a restaurant for dinner.

Today, they had spent the morning and early afternoon exploring the Pompeion and ancient Agora ruins. Having passed the outcrop of Areopagus Hill on their descent from the Acropolis the day before, they decided to return to take photos of the city below. The hill, which sat just below the

Acropolis but well above the Agora and city of Athens, afforded magnificent views.

As they ascended the path towards the Acropolis, the gradient increased, and they felt the strain on already tired legs.

"I think I've done enough walking for one day," muttered Chloe as she approached the top of the path, where it skirted the west end of the Acropolis towards the ticket offices and entrance gates.

"Climb's almost over, Chlo," noted Daphne. "It's a level path now to the hill."

As they came level with the rock, the three ladies took a turn to the right, which led to some very well-worn, shiny marble steps.

"Careful, girls," warned Tara as she began to climb the steps. "I think we need to go up here on all fours. The steps are steep and slippery."

The three friends gingerly climbed the ancient steps leading onto a flatter, glossy marble base about 25m x 80m, which was also slightly treacherous but much more manageable than the surface that they had just negotiated.

"Apparently, there was a high court here in about 500 BC," stated Tara. "They used to have murder and treason trials up here."

"I could murder a beer after that all that walking," added Daphne.

All three laughed aloud and nodded in agreement.

"We can enjoy the view for a while, then go back to that street café we went to yesterday. The one behind Hadrian's Library with the cheap beer," suggested Chloe.

"Sounds good to me, girls," added Tara with a smile.

They admired the view up towards the major structures of the Propylaea, the Erechtheion and the Parthenon on the rock above them. Below them, Athens stretched out into the distance, with the ancient Agora in the foreground. They walked around the platform area at the top of the hill, taking photos in various directions. Choosing a flat section of marble, comfortable enough to sit on, they dropped down to relax for a while.

As they took in the view, Tara noticed an unusual-looking group of people sitting talking about 10 metres away from them. There were several bohemian-looking men, one or two of whom looked like gorgeous studs! One guy looked seriously hungover. A few very elegant-looking ladies wore flowing dresses, one of whom looked very sexually stunning. A girl was in what looked like lightweight combat fatigues. She was very pretty but a bit tomboyish. Another pretty lady looked like a vampire, with jet-black hair, dark eyes, pale skin and bright red lipstick. They were an odd crew who stood apart among the other tourists.

Maybe it was because she was unintentionally staring, but one of the men had caught her eye and was smiling at her as if he knew her. He was large and muscular, with shoulder-length dark hair, a dark beard, bronzed skin, and come-to-bed blue eyes. Why was there something familiar about him?

As she watched, one of the elegant ladies slapped his face and muttered something that she couldn't hear. Then she turned her eyes towards Tara and gave her a hard stare. Tara turned away in embarrassment. Why did the woman react like that?

"I think I just upset one of the neighbours," she said quietly to Chloe and Daphne, nodding sideways towards the group of strangers.

"What? How? What did you do?" asked Daphne.

"I don't know. I was just looking at them because they looked odd. I saw one guy who looked like he was eyeing me up. Then she slapped him. Must be his wife."

"Serves him right if he's leching—right in front of his wife, too," said Chloe.

"Yes, but the odd thing is she turned and glared at me as if *I* was responsible," added Tara.

"Just ignore her, Tara," advised Daphne. "Probably just a jealous wife. Maybe he cheats on her all the time."

"Yeah, but they're making me feel uncomfortable. I don't think I want to stay up here any longer."

"No problem, Tara," said Chloe. "Let's go get that drink."

"Great idea," agreed Daphne.

"Thanks, girls," Tara said as the three stood up and moved around the rock to a metal staircase that provided a quick escape back toward the path to Monastiraki.

As the teachers exited the Areopagus Hill, Hera was giving Zeus a mouthful.

"I saw you leering at that girl, you old pervert. Why can't you ever stop your bad behaviour?"

"What girl? I was looking over towards the city below."

"You can't hide your lying eyes, you old desperado!" exclaimed Hera.

"I think I could put that to music," laughed Hermes.

"Somebody already did," added Apollo.

"You know who she was, don't you?" added Hera.

"No. Should I?" lied Zeus.

"The girl from the beach near Litochoro!"

"Really?" exclaimed Zeus, trying to look innocent. Of course he remembered her. She was actually very attractive, and she'd fed him cheese while naked.

"Don't give me that!" shouted Hera. "If I see her again, she'll be in big trouble!"

"Shouldn't it be Zeus who's in big trouble?" suggested Apollo. "After all, the girl is perfectly innocent here."

Hera snarled at Apollo, refusing to accept the truth.

"Anyway, this is a distraction," Athena pointed out. "We're here to talk about what's become of our temples and our status as gods. Can we get on with that without this childish behaviour?"

"How dare you, Athena? You can't call the king of the gods childish," snapped Hera.

"Actually, I was referring to the queen, Hera," Athena replied.

"Stop this now, ladies!" snorted Zeus. "Athena is right. This is a distraction from the reason we're all here. So, let's get down to business."

Hera glared at Athena but refrained from carrying the conversation further.

Zeus continued, "I think we all know why you organised this gathering, Athena, but maybe you'd like to give us a quick reminder?"

Athena stood up and moved back slightly so that she could address the gathered group properly, and then she began. "For hundreds of years before Homer and Hesiod told our stories, and for half a millennium afterwards, we were worshipped by the mortals of Greece and its Mediterranean colonies. People organised games and events in our honour. They prayed to us and offered up sacrifices. But in the past 2000 years, we have become almost irrelevant. People follow different religions. They have other gods or no gods at all. They have allowed our temples to fall into rubble.

"I have stood outside the Parthenon watching the crowds walk by, more obsessed with their own images and ticking their tourism visit boxes than actually appreciating the beauty and grandeur that should be the legacy of the people who built those temples.

"There are too many people coming here. They're destroying the symbols of our existence. And I think they're destroying the very nature of the planet on which they live." Scanning around the group, Athena could see that she had their attention.

Artemis commented, "It's not just here in Athens. Delos, the once grand, sacred place where we all had temples in our honour, is now a ruined town, overrun by tourists and deserted, apart from a few stray cats."

"There are also the archaeologists, Sister," Apollo pointed out. "They are trying to preserve and restore the buildings of Delos to protect them for appreciation by future generations. So, maybe that is partly in our honour?"

"No. It's in honour of the people who built the Delos community and temples. It's in honour of ancient mortals, not the Olympians," Artemis replied.

"The modern world has changed drastically in recent years," added Aphrodite. "There are far too many people. Their numbers have tripled in the last fifty years. And their technology is destroying the Earth. They have machines producing gases which choke the planet and making noises which drown out the sound of the sea and the birds singing."

"Yes, their technology has also changed warfare," added Ares. "They no longer need a god of war. Their politicians, dictators and religious leaders start wars which are fought at a distance using missiles and remotely controlled devices.

"This is my hill! Areopagus Hill. Yet if I look out across the Agora, I can see the remains of my temple. It is no more than a rectangular patch of scattered blocks placed to mark its outline. Immediately behind it is the metro line. Silver trains covered in brightly coloured graffiti scream past my temple. I'm ready to retire!" Ares finished with a sad frown.

"It isn't all bad news," said Persephone. "The more people there are, the faster the kingdom of Hades will grow as they die. And the proliferation of deadly weapons will help to accelerate that."

"Alcoholic drinks aren't doing too badly either," noted Dionysus. "There are more alternatives available all the time, and most people are enjoying them."

"But it's not you who is controlling the proliferation of alcohol, Dionysus," added Hephaestus. "Once again, it's human ingenuity. You may have started the process, but it is the march of technology and science which has led to the massive variety and quantity of drinks available."

"If you look across the Agora, over to the left of my brother, Ares' temple, you'll see one fine, complete building, with its low pointed roof and Doric columns. That's my temple," Hephaestus stated proudly. "The best-preserved temple in all of Greece!"

"I suppose that's what we should expect, my son," said Zeus. "In honour of the god of craftsmanship, the most solidly crafted of all the temples. The only building in the Agora that is in better condition is the Stoa of Attalos, but that isn't preserved. It was reconstructed just 60 years ago. A replica of the ancient building."

"The Stoa was the commercial hub of ancient Athens," Hermes said. "That it has been reconstructed in modern times is a tribute to business and commerce, which I will claim is in honour of the god of merchants, tricksters and thieves. Commerce makes the mortal world go round, so I guess that is a success story," he concluded with a confident grin.

Apollo added, "The reason the Temple of Hephaestus is in such good condition is that it was used as a Greek Orthodox church for more than one thousand years. It was the church of St. George until just two hundred years ago and was a museum for a long time after that. That's why it is well maintained, not because the modern Greeks love Hephaestus!"

"You've burst my bubble, Apollo!" Hephaestus responded with a frown.

"You think that restoring divine intervention will somehow return us to our future glory, Athena," said Apollo. "But that would surely depend on how we intervene. The archaeologists and technical experts are doing their best to preserve or reconstruct the ancient buildings. However, as Artemis mentioned, that is preserving the legacy of the ancient craftsmen, not honouring their gods."

"Athena, you broke the rules when you squeezed the bladder of an American tourist outside the Parthenon," said Hera. "Did that help to restore your former glory?"

"No, but it felt good," Athena admitted. "Anyway, he deserved it. He was leering at my breasts."

"So how do you think divine intervention would help?" asked Apollo.

"Watching what has been happening to Athens over the years, I just thought that the human world is turning into a mess and that we need to take some major action to correct that."

"Most human politicians would say the same thing," observed Zeus. "I think before we even think about where we should or shouldn't intervene, we need to dig a little bit deeper. There are some questions we need to consider. For example, who were the ancient Greeks? Why did they worship us in the way that they did? Why did mortals lose faith in us and allow our temples to decay? Let's reflect on these questions for a few minutes.

"Just look around. Think back 2500 years to when the Parthenon was built. Imagine all the scenery, the great edifices of the Propylaea, the Erechtheion, the temples and markets of the Agora, and the Greek people going about their business. We are sitting up here at the high court on the Areopagus.

"Now look at the expanse of modern Athens stretching into the distance, away from the ancient sites—five million people living in a city which also attracts many tourists. The world has changed. People's lives and capabilities have changed. But they are still in awe of the ancient Greeks and their mythology. To understand our own fall from grace, we need to step back and think objectively."

The gods all reflected on Zeus's advice. Individually, they scanned the panorama before them. The strange mix of ancient ruins and modern city. The hustle and bustle of Monastiraki and the streets beyond the Agora. How and why should they intervene to change any of this? Was there some ideal state of the world that they should strive to return to, or should they simply accept that their own demise was part of the natural progress of the world and humanity?

Chapter 13: The Ancient Greeks

"So, Father," Athena queried, "why is it that the ancient Greeks assembled all of those wonderful buildings? Particularly the great temples in our honour that have since been allowed to crumble to ruins?"

"Well, Athena, first you have to ask who the people were who did that construction. Why did they think they needed to build the temples?" Zeus asked.

"Mythology tells us they were the first people who lived in Athens," Athena answered. "Descendants of the first men, who were shaped out of clay for your entertainment, by Prometheus. The people into whom I breathed life and personality. The men to whom Prometheus eventually gave fire, against your will!"

"Yes, the men to whom Hephaestus then gifted Pandora. A companion whose shape was modelled on yourself and my sisters, Hera, Aphrodite and Demeter. The first woman into whom Aphrodite breathed life and the art of love. To whom Hermes gave guile and cunning, and Hera gave grace. All of the gods gave her the qualities to be a perfect partner throughout the life of a man," said Zeus.

"It was you, Zeus," interrupted Apollo, "who tricked Pandora by giving her a box of secrets which she was told never to open. Your cunning revenge on Prometheus for giving man fire against your will was to destroy humanity. You knew Pandora would open the box, releasing all the evils of pestilence, hatred and war, leaving only hope trapped inside."

Zeus sighed, "Yes, my son. That is the story as told by mythology. But there are those who would tell you an alternative story: a scientific explanation of the origins of both humanity and the ancient Greeks."

"Does it affect my wish for divine intervention to be reinstated?" asked Athena.

"I believe it does," replied Zeus. "Should I tell you the story?"

Athena nodded reluctantly, anticipating that the outcome would not be in her favour.

"Well, gods and goddesses," he said, glancing around the group of immortals on the Areopagus Hill. "The scientists will tell you that humans were not shaped from clay by either Prometheus or Hephaestus. They were part of an ever-changing web of life, which began more than three billion years ago, when very simple creatures, made of protein and RNA, showed the ability to replicate themselves to produce a new generation of offspring. The offspring changed over time, becoming ever more complex as nature selected the individuals with the best characteristics for passing on to each generation.

“This process of evolution was driven forward by changing conditions in the seas and on the land to eventually produce all of the living creatures that have occupied the planet. Humanity is just one of those creatures which evolved as part of the natural processes of life.

“The shape of coastlines and landscapes is dynamic; perpetually in motion. The Earth’s surface is made from great tectonic plates that are continually shifting, pushing up mountains, and creating new valleys. Across the eons, regional climates have continually changed: sometimes very slowly, sometimes noticeably within a lifetime. Today’s deserts were not always dry, and today’s wetlands were not always wet. Rivers have grown and shrunk, depending on the climate in their catchments, and have cut new pathways through hills and across floodplains, searching for the best route to the oceans.

“Humanity did not begin in Greece. People evolved from ape-like ancestors in equatorial East Africa, where they hunted other animals for food and skins. During the last few million years, they moved out of forests onto savannah grasslands and open plains in pursuit of grazing animal herds. Their hunting prowess improved along with their communication and cooperation skills. They became more upright, larger-brained and more intelligent. They learned to turn natural materials into tools and weapons. They learned how to control fire, cook and harden tools and weapons.

"The evolution of human intelligence had a very important prerequisite trait. Curiosity! In order to learn and develop new ideas, man needed to want answers and to solve problems. Curiosity raised many questions in the human mind. Where did we come from? How did we get here? Where do we go when we die? Are our ancestors there already? Will we meet them again?

"The world in which they lived presented its own particular characteristics to the curious mind. What was the bright light that moved across the sky every day? What caused the thunder and lightning that frequently accompanied rainstorms? Why did the Earth sometimes shake and tremble or shoot hot rocks and ash into the air? What monsters were in the wide expanses of deep water, often swept by storm waves and strong winds?"

"Mythology answers all these questions for them," interrupted Hermes. "Why did they need an alternative?"

"They didn't. It was the early humans who created mythology in order to answer the questions they couldn't answer," replied Zeus. "The scientific answers have only come to light over the last few centuries.

"The first early-human creatures had migrated from Africa onto the Arabian Peninsula a million years ago, when geographical landscapes, food and water supplies had enabled them to follow prey animals along coastlines and river valleys. From the Arabian Peninsula, they were to gradually spread in small groups across Asia and Europe, sometimes separated by periods of thousands or tens of thousands of years.

"The hunter-gatherer groups who migrated to the north, east and west were usually small tribes or large family groups of about a few dozen to a few hundred people. At first, they had simply followed their prey, living from hunting, fishing and foraging for edible plants, berries and nuts as they moved around.

"As climatic conditions and food availability changed, there were plentiful periods when the human population would increase and move into new territories. In more difficult times, food became scarcer and tribal groups competed for fewer resources. Sometimes, they would come into conflict, fighting for access to terrain and to prey herds. Often, the victors would murder defeated males and take the females into their tribes, initially as slaves or war booty. Over time, the slaves would be integrated into the tribe, mixing their genes into a new, modified population. But the number of individuals in a tribe, and the total population of a region, was always restricted by the availability of food, water and shelter."

"Isn't this story supposed to be about the ancient Greeks, Zeus?" asked Hephaestus.

"I will come to that, Hephaestus, but in order to understand how the first people settled in Greece, it helps if you know who their ancestors were. Greece didn't just begin with ancient cities and temples.

"Over the past 400,000 years, there was a series of very cold ice ages, when ice sheets had crept southwards from the Arctic and downwards from high mountain peaks into the valleys of central Europe. At such times, the human population was pushed back into low-lying areas. There were small pockets of people in warmer refuges scattered around the milder areas of Europe. Sea levels were also lower, so people settled into areas around coastlines and river valleys that would later be flooded by the rising sea.

"Throughout the last ice age, among the largest refuges for human populations were the Fertile Crescent region between the Tigris and Euphrates rivers, and adjacent lands to the East of the Mediterranean and South of the Caucasus Mountains. The last cold period came to an end about 12,000 years ago. As the weather conditions changed and more food became available, the population in the refuges grew relatively rapidly. During the first few millennia of the warming period, people learned to enclose livestock. Goats, sheep, cattle and pigs became food sources that they could manage and exploit. In addition, they discovered how to grow and manage plant crops, such as wheat.

"As farming developed, people began to build settlements. Small village communities became the focal points for domestication and management of food species and for a more sedentary type of life. As community sizes expanded, new land was needed for food production, and additional settlements were sought for human expansion. Waves of people radiated out from the Fertile Crescent and Eastern Mediterranean. They migrated around coasts, up rivers, and over mountain passes, taking farming techniques with them.

"Between 10,000 and 5,000 BC, small groups of people arrived in Greece from different directions. Some came around the southern and western Anatolian coastline, often crossing the sea to settle on the many islands of the Aegean. Others came around the northern Anatolian Black Sea coast, crossing from the Bosphorus and Sea of Marmara to the northern Aegean and northern Greece. Yet others had travelled around the north of the Black Sea, through the Caucasus Mountains and across the Ukrainian Steppe grasslands, entering Greece from the lands to the north.

"The southern group were seafarers, who brought sheep and goats with them to the southern Aegean and Crete. The northern Anatolian group brought cattle and cereal farming. The tribes from the Steppes included men on horseback. People who witnessed the arrival of men on horses in the region spread stories of the Centaurs—creatures that were half man, half horse—vicious warriors who fired arrows as they galloped towards their victims.

"Many tribal settlements appeared in different parts of Greece and the Aegean islands. Their ancestral origins varied. They spoke different languages. They had different base cultures and varied genetic origins. Although they usually continued to hunt some animals, such as wild boar or deer, the survival of expanding settled communities had come to rely on farming and access to local wild food plants and water supplies.

"As the settlements grew, they would sometimes clash with others and do battle. Villages became fortified and required protection by militias and armies. Small villages grew into cities, usually governed by a ruling dynasty, warlord, or king. By the start of the Bronze Age, around 3000 BC, Greece had become a collection of small, independent kingdoms, each based on a ruling city, the best known of which was Athens. Sometimes trading, sometimes at war, the Greek kingdoms co-existed in ever-changing alliances for several thousand years.

"Copper deposits in Anatolia and the Balkans enabled the development of bronze as a metal for ornamental, utility and weaponry uses. During the Bronze Age, the Aegean region was dominated by the Minoan Kingdom until the eruption of the Santorini volcano around 1600 BC. Most of the Minoan settlements were buried in ashes or swamped by tsunamis.

"On mainland Anatolia, near the Sea of Marmara, Troy became the dominant kingdom of the northeastern Aegean. Its easy access to Anatolian copper and large expanses of fertile land for farming allowed Troy to become a very wealthy city. Its importance as a regional trading centre continued into the late Bronze Age until it was destroyed in a prolonged war against an alliance of Greek kingdoms around 1200 BC.

"What about the temples? And us gods? Where do the scientists say that we come into the story?" asked Hermes.

"Well, my son Hermes, they say that we gods evolved in the minds of mortals over the last forty thousand years or more. Curious people came up with their own explanations for aspects of life. These explanations were turned into stories told around campfires, changing slowly as they were coloured by the storytellers. There were people living in Athens from well before 2000 BC, but the ruins you can see today were all built after 1000 BC. There may have been earlier temples to us gods, but it seems that the early Greeks created us Olympians in their own image!"

"According to the scientists!" noted Hera loudly, making her opinion clear.

"The ancient stories of gods, kings and heroes had been told by poets and sung by musicians for several hundred years since the events of the Trojan War. The stories were gradually contorted, embellished and exaggerated until Hesiod and Homer froze them in ink around 700 BC.

"Whether Helen, queen of Sparta, was actually kidnapped and taken to Troy by Prince Paris may never be verified. More likely, political jealousies and greed may have led to the onslaught and the 10-year war that followed. The story told in Homer's Iliad was written 500 years after the event. The Iliad tells of battles between warriors, princes, kings and heroes in a conflict manipulated and influenced by us gods.

"At the end of the war, Homer told of Odysseus's 10-year journey, beset by disasters, monsters, witches and the gradual loss of his men and their ships. King Menelaus of Sparta was shipwrecked on his way back to Sparta. Agamemnon of Mycenae, who had led the Greeks, was murdered by his wife Clytemnestra on return from the war. However, Mycenae eventually became the most important city-state in the late Bronze Age for a few hundred years before all of the Greek city-states fell into decline—a dark age in ancient Greek history.

"Possibly, the Greek kingdoms fell from grace after destroying the Trojans, just as the Roman Empire would eventually collapse into a dark age from the height of its importance 1000 years later. Homer's poetry in the Iliad and Odyssey, although covering 20 years of events, may have symbolised the destruction of Troy and the subsequent collapse of the Greek alliance over a period of several centuries.

"The Greek city-states rose in importance once again in the early Iron Age, around 800 BC. During the dark years, the seafaring Phoenicians sailed from Tyre and Sidon on the coast of what is now Lebanon to colonise new settlements. They traded increasingly with the Greeks as they travelled across the Mediterranean. Around this time, the Greek Cyrillic alphabet, derived from the script used by the Phoenicians, became the basis of written records.

"Hesiod wrote the story of the origin of the gods, the creation of man, and the adventures of the ancient heroes. Homer told the story of the Trojan War and the wanderings of Odysseus. The personalities and stories that had evolved through centuries of poetry became defined in a form which would remain unchanged until modern times. However, what these authors have done is to record our personalities from stories written around 700 BC for perpetuity!

"That's a long and complex story, Father," said Athena. "I think we need to go and obtain some refreshments before continuing. We still have to discuss my request to allow divine intervention once more, now that we've all seen the state of the temples and the crowds of tourists."

"I'll second that," said Dionysus. "There's a nice little taverna on Adrianou, just behind Hadrian's Library, where we can have a cold beer and some meze."

The gods arose from the marble rocks on which they had been sitting and walked down the metal stairway towards the path back to Monastiraki. Ten minutes later, they arrived at Adrianou.

On the street below the taverna, about twenty tables, each with four chairs, stood on a wide, paved area beside the boundary wall of Hadrian's Library. About half of the tables were already in use. The gods found three adjacent, unoccupied tables and sat down to wait for service.

Separated from the gods by a few occupied tables, Tara lowered her head and placed her hands in front of her face. "Oh no! It's those people again. Please don't let her see me!" Tara muttered quietly.

Daphne and Chloe glanced towards the group, who were now sitting, talking and laughing, a little bit closer than the teachers would have preferred.

"Just don't let her catch your eye, Tara," said Chloe. "They don't have any reason to pick on us."

For a few minutes, the gods were distracted by ordering drinks and items from the meze menu. They chatted together while being served. Hera wasn't directly facing the girls, so she hadn't noticed them, but unfortunately, Zeus was looking in their direction. His eyes lit up as he spotted the three girls from the beach near Mount Olympus. Characteristically, he began trying to eye them up while sitting next to Hera, but without her noticing.

"Oh no! The unfaithful husband has spotted us," groaned Daphne, glancing indirectly towards where Zeus, Hera, Athena and Persephone were sharing a table.

Zeus's excitement grew. It seemed that he and the teachers were fated to cross paths, but how could he arrange an encounter with them in the presence of Hera and the other Olympians?

Persephone noticed that Zeus was smiling sideways past Hera at somebody behind her. Innocently, she turned around to look and noticed Daphne glancing sideways and Tara trying to hide her face.

"Is that somebody you know, Zeus?" Persephone enquired.

"What? Who? No, I don't think so." Zeus muttered unconvincingly.

Alerted to Zeus's gaze towards the girls, Hera turned her head and spotted them. She glared at each of the three in turn, her face darkening and eyes closing angrily.

"I think this is time for some serious divine intervention," she growled.

Concerned at Hera's unfair, jealous reaction, Athena put her hand on her stepmother's shoulder.

“Please, Hera, those ladies haven’t done anything wrong. They’re simply having a drink without seeking any attention. If anybody should experience your wrath, it should be Zeus.”

“Well, husband!” snapped Hera. “What do you have to say for yourself?”

“My dear wife, I haven’t done anything wrong. Maybe I unconsciously recognised those ladies, but I haven’t approached them in any way. It’s just a coincidence that they have turned up here in Athens.”

“I’ll be watching your every moment and movement, Zeus. I know you too well!”

Meanwhile, Tara, Chloe and Daphne had hurried to finish their drinks. They stood up and walked back to the taverna to pay, keeping as considerable a distance as possible between themselves and the gods.

“Very strange behaviour, if you ask me,” said Chloe. That old guy fancies Tara, leers at her, and his wife then glares at us as if we’re encouraging it!”

“It takes all sorts, girls,” said Daphne. “Hopefully, that’s the last we’ll see of them.”

They strolled down into Monastiraki Square, browsing the souvenir shops and sampling street food. They sat on a low wall eating souvlaki wraps and then ice creams while watching the colourful cosmopolitan crowds pass slowly through the square. Street hustlers dressed as Disney characters tried to dance with bypassing tourists, hoping to persuade them to pay for photo poses. Street musicians and jugglers played to the crowds.

"I think it best to hold your bags tight around here," said Daphne.

"Yes, it's probably a pickpocket's paradise here," added Tara.

"Also, watch out for the bum-pinchers!" laughed Chloe.

"I think we've already met one of those, with his jealous wife!" said Tara, laughing heartily.

"It's been a lovely day, girls, despite the encounter with those strange people," said Daphne.

"Aye, it's a shame we have to go home tomorrow," noted Chloe. "Time to go and relax for an hour or two, then we can go out and try one of those rooftop cocktail bars tonight. That should be a lovely end to our little trip to Greece."

Clutching their day bags protectively, they wound their way through the meandering tourists who filled Monastiraki Square, heading back to their hotel for a shower and a nap before the final night of their holiday.

Chapter 14: Figments of the Imagination

Once the three teachers had disappeared from their street table by the taverna, Athena and Persephone had managed to convince Hera that she had been overreacting to their presence. As always, she had vented her anger on the potential victims of Zeus's lust. However, now, they were out of sight and almost out of mind.

The eleven gods present were gathered around three tables, away from the other restaurant customers. They could talk freely and privately. Athena decided to take the opportunity to continue the discussion about the reasons they were having this reunion.

"So, Father, will you agree to reintroduce divine intervention?" asked Athena.

"Well, it seemed to work before: in mythology, within the stories of the heroes, and during the Trojan War. We have all played our part in shaping Greek mythology by intervening directly in human affairs, myself included," stated Zeus.

"Then reinstate it. That's the consensus among the Olympians, Father," added Artemis.

"Is it now? Hades isn't here. Poseidon isn't here. Hestia and Demeter are against it. I don't think those who are here are all in agreement. Ares, Athena, Aphrodite, Artemis, you are the only ones who really care about this. However, how would you actually use divine powers for the better? Would you intervene in politics? Start wars? Stop wars? Frighten people into worshipping you?"

"We could drastically change the weather around the world," suggested Hermes. "Create major storms, big freezes and very hot periods. Droughts will produce food shortages and famines. They may call on the gods to help them."

"The mortals don't need us gods to do the things you're suggesting," Zeus said. "Their activities are changing the chemistry of the atmosphere. As time proceeds, they are already creating ever more dramatic storms. It's raining when it should be sunny, and there are droughts when there should be rain. They're forever changing the environment upon which nature depends. These factors are destroying their food crops."

"Maybe we could create a great flood like the ancient one. Raise the level of the seas to drown all of the settlements, farms and commercial centres on coastal plains," said Hephaestus.

"The warming atmosphere is already melting the Earth's ice caps and glaciers, raising the sea level," explained Zeus. "Remember the end of the last ice age, eight to ten thousand years ago? The sea level rose nearly 200 metres. In some centuries, it rose 2.5 metres. People saw their coastal settlements gradually sinking into the seas. The storytellers created myths about how us gods had sent a great flood to punish humanity for not paying us sufficient homage. But the truth is, we did not send the flood. It was a result of the creeping changes of nature. Humanity had self-inflicted punishment for building on coastal plains during the ice age. Such stories added to the foundations of mythology, which elevated us to important symbols of nature."

"We could up the supply of alcoholic drinks and maybe some more toxic substances. Drive them all into crazy intoxication," said Dionysos, smiling. "Life could be one big party, and maybe they'd all worship the grapevine."

"How about spreading some fatal diseases?" suggested Apollo. "Like when Artemis stopped the wind and sent a plague to the ships of the Greek alliance to prevent them departing to attack Troy."

"Agamemnon had shot a sacred stag. I demanded recompense," agreed Artemis.

"You demanded the sacrifice of his daughter Iphigenia!" added Hera. "That was a bit harsh to take her life for a stag."

"I didn't. I swapped her for a stag on the sacrificial altar and took her in as a handmaiden," argued Artemis. "Anyway, that worked. Agamemnon agreed to sacrifice his own daughter to appease me, the huntress, for having killed my stag."

"New diseases appear all the time," Zeus said. "Human population density and their movements between different countries and big cities ensures illnesses spread without any help from the gods. We have no need to intervene. Nature already provides multiple routes to human death."

"But that's exactly *why* we need divine intervention," Athena stated. "If the only things affecting the progress of humanity are natural processes, then we need to use supernatural powers if we want to change anything."

"What do you want to change? And, what exactly should those powers be?" asked Zeus. "Should I direct thunderbolts at political leaders? I suppose I could blast Putin before he blasts the planet."

Athena responded, "We have lost our status and dignity as deities. We want to restore that. Regarding how we should use divine powers, we could act together as a council. No individual god should take matters into their own hands. We should always follow the guidance of the council. In particular, your opinion, Father. And Apollo's Oracle."

"Wise words, my dear," said Zeus, "but Apollos's Oracle? Really? Maybe the Trojans should have listened to Casandra. Her predictions were always more precise than the Oracle. The Oracle is about as reliable as a newspaper astrology entry."

"But my advice as the Oracle and the curses on ancient families featured in many of the stories of Greek mythology," Apollo interjected.

"And the key word here is mythology! We, ourselves, are a part of mythology. We don't actually exist!"

"How can we be having this conversation if we don't exist?" asked Hermes.

"We don't exist as physical entities. We have no presence in the real world. However, as mythological beings, we exist in the minds of men. We are figments of the imagination. We exist in the imagination of the storyteller and his listeners, of the author and his readers. But close the book, and we are gone. We are all just figments of the imagination."

"How can that be, Father?" queried Ares. "Why would we be simply imagined? We are complex beings with real personalities."

"Indeed, my son. Mankind has a vivid imagination. Vivid, but not necessarily clever. Men are inclined to create gods in their own images. They need explanations for the complexities of life. They need answers to some simple questions. How? When? Where? Why? Who?

"And of course, we are the answer to the question, 'Who?' If they don't have an answer to this question, then it must have been the gods who did it.

"They also needed to have stories that answer the question 'How?' Those are the myths that were written down by Homer and Hesiod all those years ago. But when they wrote down the myths, they trapped our personalities along with their contemporary view of our deeds. Our story became one big soap opera, telling all about our deeds, good or bad, exposing our personalities, strengths and weaknesses, and our relationships, even when those were inappropriate.

"And don't forget the question 'When?' Our mythology was imagined at a time before civilisation. We are the third generation of immortals. Before us, there were the Titans, and before that, there was just Gaia, the Earth, and Ouranus, the Sky.

"Gaia and Ouranus had been born out of chaos but gave birth to the Titans. It was the Titan, Kronos, who castrated Ouranus and threw his genitals into the sea, where they transformed into Aphrodite, the first of us Olympian gods. The rest of us are the children or grandchildren of Kronos.

"Before civilisation, the only things that mattered to people were birth, death, food, water, sex and shelter. So, the first gods they imagined were the god of sex, Aphrodite, the god of the dead, Hades, and the god controlling thunder and lighting, myself. And, of course, the god who makes the ground shake and causes storms at sea, Poseidon.

"This is the pantheon, which people already believed in before they had settlements or villages. They witnessed nature and feared its forces, storms, the deep blue sea and death. Life was all about sex and survival. There was no civilisation. No complex rules, just their basic instincts for survival within an extended family group. This was the system within which the first of the gods were created.

"However, even as nomadic hunters without permanent settlements, people told stories of their experiences and exploits beside the campfire. This was the hearth, the focus of family life and hospitality. The hearth became the domain of Hestia. With the arrival of settlements and the evolution of village life, the hearth became the focus of the homestead."

"Why isn't Hestia here with us then?" asked Ares. "As one of the older members of the pantheon, her opinion should have been important in this debate."

Persephone responded to Ares as Hestia's proxy, "We have Hestia's opinion. She is happy to symbolise hospitality in every household. It is something which should be given freely by the occupants to their guests, not an intervention from the gods. She sees no need for temples, as every hearth is her temple."

Zeus continued his explanation. "With the beginning of farming came the god responsible for ensuring the annual regrowth of food plants. Demeter joined the pantheon in this role. But she lamented in the dark months of the year because, as the myths had explained, her daughter Persephone had to take her place as queen of the underworld for half of the year. Demeter would only allow plants to grow when Persephone returned in the spring."

"But the warm and cold seasons had always existed before people had farming settlements," Artemis noted.

"True, Daughter. However, it was with the need to understand farming that an explanation for the seasons became important. This was more apparent when people spread into temperate climates in Europe, where there were large differences between summer and winter weather," Zeus replied.

"My mother, Demeter, is in agreement with Hestia. We symbolise the seasons," said Persephone. "We don't need divine intervention for people to love the regrowth in the spring and to be saddened by the short, dark, cold days of winter."

"Your husband, Hades, isn't here, Persephone," noted Zeus. "Would the king of the underworld call for divine intervention?"

"Nobody can avoid death. Most fear it or are resigned to accepting it. But my husband, Hades, has no need to intervene in life. All mortals will come to him eventually."

"And what about the three minstrels? No musical instruments to cheer us after these dark thoughts from Persephone?" asked Zeus.

"Your story of the pantheon hasn't mentioned us yet, Zeus," noted Hermes.

"Not yet," Zeus concurred. "You three were late arrivals on the scene. As villages grew and became cities, there were people with new functions: traders, craftsmen, people who could make tools, farming implements, and weapons. Hephaestus joined the pantheon as the representative of metal workers and craftsmen. Hermes represented traders, businessmen and thieves. And all this work made them thirsty. Dionysus joined the rest of us after people discovered how to make wine and beer."

Ares glanced at his father, Zeus, wondering whether his angry, aggressive personality merited a mention in the history of the Olympians.

Catching his eye and reading his thoughts, Zeus added, "With the availability of weapons and farming communities to protect, wars became inevitable. Fighting demanded rage to drive warriors into close combat. Each fighter assumed he had the support of an immortal war god who was firing up his anger and directing the thrust of his weapon."

"What about us twins, Father?" asked Artemis. "What model were we created from?"

"You go back to before civilisation, to the hunter-gatherer community. You, Artemis, represent something pure found in teenage girls when they are coming of age, still capable of firing an arrow or hunting in the forest. Still virginal and without children. You represent a youthful energy that would be stolen from a girl once she has become a mother, and her life then needed to be devoted to raising children.

"Apollo, too, was the spirit of youth. A hunter, but also clever and talented. In the early community, he represented the young man, not the father figure, but a growing spirit who would come to the fore in the future. He could predict the future. He could heal the sick, play music and sing. Apollo was the god of newly acquired knowledge—a hope for the future. Yet, he was also a powerful athlete who would be a role model for the growing youth in a community.

"All of our roles and personality traits were the tools of ancient storytellers. They told of a powerful, immortal family who were responsible for the way in which the world and humanity worked together."

"Why then, Father, did people stop believing in us and worshipping us as deities?" asked Athena.

"As I mentioned, men created us in their own image. The pantheon and the characters of the Olympians evolved alongside early civilisation, but only until the stories were written down around 700 BC. Once that had been done, our characters were set in stone. We could no longer evolve. Because we had been imagined by pre-civilisation people, we did not have the morals and follow the rules of civilised people. Our behaviour was inappropriate."

"Yours, more so than the rest of us," interrupted Hera. "Today, you would be considered to be a bisexual, paedophilic, incestuous rapist!"

"That's a bit strong coming from my loving wife!" noted Zeus. "Perhaps, my dear, you would acknowledge that your own behaviour would not be considered correct for that of a queen today. For all of my flawed liaisons, it's always my victims that you seek to punish. You seek out those with whom I've had relations and take out your spiteful revenge on them."

Artemis added, "Yes, Hera. You tried to prevent myself and Apollo from being born and then tried to kill us. But we didn't have sex with Zeus. We were just the result of his seduction of our own mother."

"And as for *me* being incestuous, Hera, my love, I should remind you that I am not only your husband, I am also your brother. The thing to remember is that the stories were written before the rules of civilisation. So, we represent a dynasty from the earliest farming communities. The stories written about us applied standards of behaviour that may have been acceptable in the Bronze Age. A village elder or tribal leader might have been able to pick and choose among the developing girls of the community with impunity. But if he had overstepped the accepted rules of his tribe, then maybe he would have been overthrown. This is exactly the type of story repeated throughout Greek mythology."

"We're all far from innocent," added Hera, seeking to point the finger away from herself. Take you, Aphrodite. You promised Helen, the queen of Mycenae, who was married to Menelaus, as a prize for Paris, prince of Troy. That was just a bribe to make him say you were more beautiful than either Athena or myself."

“I don’t think I needed to bribe him, Hera. He could have seen for himself that I was the fairest of the goddesses,” said Aphrodite.

Hera hissed at Aphrodite contemptuously.

“I’m beginning to see my father’s point here,” said Athena. “Without Aphrodite’s bribe of Paris, there wouldn’t have been a Trojan War. We’re all just pawns in the storyteller’s soap opera. But our characters are not what would have been acceptable for gods in a more advanced society.”

“None of you are perfect,” said Hera. “Apollo gave Casandra the ability to see the future, then spat in her mouth and cursed her never to be believed. If they’d listened to her, the Trojans could have won.”

“Casandra went back on a promise to have sex with me!” said Apollo, expecting that to be accepted as an excuse.

“Exactly! That shows just how good a role model you really are for maturing youths,” said Hera.

“The worrying thing is,” added Zeus, “that we were created in the image of man. Our behaviour was accepted as that of a ruling dynasty in the years before civilisation changed the rules. That implies that the behaviour of the Greek gods is modelled on that of early settled communities. In other words, our behaviour reflects that of basic human nature. We behave in the same way that a ruling family might, as a result of their innate desires and instincts."

"That might explain why people stopped worshipping us," observed Hermes. "As human societies became more complex, then legal systems and ethical practices became important in order to control and manage behaviour. Otherwise, communities might have behaved irrationally. Without basic rules, theft, violence, rape and murder would have been rife, simply because people could behave according to their instinctive desires. Without moral guidance, biological impulses would have taken control. That would have been total anarchy!"

"That's exactly correct, Hermes," said Athena. "A few hundred years after the myths were written down by Homer and Hesiod, Plato and Socrates were telling people that the stories of the Gods had been based on stories about real people and that their behaviour had been primitive. The Greeks continued to have games and celebrations at the temples, in our honour as a tradition. But these were social gatherings. The gods became more symbolic of aspects of life, rather than representing real characters. For example, I was the symbol of the city of Athens. When the Romans came to dominate, they continued to celebrate us, the Olympian gods, but eventually began to ignore us while they deified some of their own

Emperors. To the Roman Empire, Tiberias and Claudius were gods, despite their appalling behaviour.

"Yes, Daughter," said Zeus. "Complex societies needed rules, and the old gods weren't acceptable role models, so mortals created new religions in which they believed there was a single, all-powerful force for good, which had created humanity. By following the rules set by the followers of these religions, they would, in principle, lead a correct path through life's obstacles.

"Furthermore, although some people might argue, and even believe, that they have witnessed supernatural events, there is no proof that anything supernatural has ever happened beyond the imagination of the supposed witness," affirmed Zeus.

"In other words, supernatural things do not happen. The very term supernatural means above the laws of nature. While humanity's laws may be there to be broken, nature's laws cannot be, which means that any form of divine intervention cannot exist except as a figment of the imagination. When Homer wrote the Iliad, he described many such instances during the Trojan War. However, these events were recounted in the imagination of the storyteller and absorbed by his audience."

Zeus paused and glanced around the gathering, now silenced in contemplation of his statements.

"So, my dear Athena, I can happily reinstate divine intervention, but in the real 21st-century world, I don't think we will see the course of human progress altered in any direction by supernatural events."

Athena considered Zeus's point, then added, "Maybe we can't use divine intervention to change humanity, but is there some way we can reinstate ourselves as an immortal pantheon, deserving worship and respect?"

"Well, my dear, most people are a bit like sheep. They need a shepherd or shepherds to follow and a few dogs to direct them. If there were enough enjoyable stories written about the Olympians and why they are great role models, then some people might be daft enough to believe in us. It would probably take more than books. Some movies and the odd TV series would help, maybe?

"However, 21st-century man already has his pantheon of gods. He watches their activities on screens, at home, in the cinema, or in sports stadiums. Some of them play games, kicking or throwing balls around to score points. Others might be musicians, or actors playing the roles of superheroes. Whatever their particular powers, huge flocks of people are prepared to baaaa to them. They pay large sums of money to watch them in the stadiums and arenas while the shepherds get rich and the dogs are well-fed on their scraps.

"We, the Olympians, are soap opera characters, imagined from before civilisation seriously took hold. We showed all the basic human emotions and behaviours, good and bad, which might have been normal before there were any social rules. Every time there is war or conflict between modern people, we still hear of the worst excesses committed by soldiers against civilians and refugees. They commit rape, torture and murder, acts against the rules of civilisation, but often ingrained into their instinctive behaviour and enacted if they think there will be no consequences. If there are no witnesses to their deeds, then there is usually no justice or recompense.

"People have not changed, but civilisation gradually introduced ethics and justice. Unfortunately, our own behaviour in mythology predated ethics and justice. We were not good enough to be more modern gods.

"People enjoy stories, myths and fables. They want to have explanations for their own feelings and guidance on what equates to good or bad behaviour. They can normally judge that instinctively, but they don't necessarily comply with their own instincts. It was necessary for civilisation to develop social rules which could be policed.

"Today, despite the hindsight provided by history and the knowledge of civilisation's social and moral codes, people still enjoy hearing bad news and watching soap operas describing the misfortune of others. Stories of murder, corruption, evil and horror are firm favourites for pacifying the 21st-century sheep. We were the original models."

"So, you are saying, Zeus," said Hermes, "that we can use divine intervention in an imaginary situation, such as a story, because it would not be real?"

"That's the bottom line," replied Zeus.

"Are you happy with that, Athena?" asked Hera.

"Well, it's not what I had hoped for, but my father, Zeus, has given us some serious food for thought."

"Do you realise that I spend six months of the year as queen of the dead?" Persephone pointed out to the assembled gods. "I haven't seen most of you for thousands of years, but now we're all gathered together in Athens," she added with a smile.

"Yes, I think it's party time," said Apollo, twiddling his laurel wreath pendant.

Athena groaned, "How many times did I tell you all that this wasn't supposed to be a party? We're here to talk about how we restore our status and dignity."

"Well, we can all use our imagination; we can imagine the best party ever, with divine intervention if we choose it," laughed Aphrodite.

Ares managed to smile while imagining ways to sneak Aphrodite away from the party.

"I think enough has been said of our place in the world," said Zeus. "Athena, I think you need to accept that the consensus is that we should enjoy this reunion. We can reflect on how the world has changed and hopefully accept it. If we can influence the future, whether via our actions or through our influence on the imagination of others, then so be it. But for now, let's make the most of our time together."

Nodding in agreement, the gathered Olympians finished their drinks at the Adrianou Taverna and then strolled off together to explore the back streets between the Acropolis and Monastiraki.

Shuffling through the milling crowds, they passed by many shops with colourful windows and street displays. Coloured garments, books, souvenirs, street food and cafes lined the district pavements.

Pausing in front of a row of shops, Zeus turned to face Athena, "Tell me, Daughter, what do you notice about the goods on sale at these shops?"

Athena glanced from shop front to shop front before responding, “Well, they’re mostly tourist shops selling things the local people don’t need: guidebooks, silly toys, figurines and statues, T-shirts and dresses, street food and ice cream.”

“Look more closely at the contents, Athena. Who are the figurines? What are the books about? What’s on the T-shirts?” he added.

“The figurines are mainly of us Olympians,” Athena noted.

“Exactly, Athena!” Zeus responded. There are hundreds, or even thousands of little idols of us Greek gods being sold all over Athens and in the rest of Greece.”

“But these aren’t for the Greeks. They’re tourist souvenirs. They’re for people to take back to their home countries as souvenirs or presents,” observed Hermes.

“Yes, but why would they do that if they don’t hold us in awe for some reason?” asked Zeus. “They may not pray to us or offer sacrifices, but they hold us in a strange, sentimental respect, despite our personalities. The Greeks may not be buying them, but they are selling them. They’re using our images to promote Greece and its historic culture, and bring money into their economy. Would they do that if we didn’t mean something significant and special?

"Look around," Zeus continued. "The books are either about the ancient sites and temples or about Greek mythology. People want to read about us.

"And look at the T-shirts. What are the pictures on the front? They're either symbols of Athens, Greece, or pictures of us gods!"

"Some of them are sports shirts with names on. Mbappe, Messe!" Hermes pointed out.

"Ah, of course. These are some of the modern gods. The ones they like to worship in stadiums and TV screens," added Zeus.

"I can see my dress hanging in lots of shops," noted Athena.

"Of course, my dear, because you are beautiful in that dress. It's a perfect holiday dress for watching the sun go down outside a beach taverna on one of our beautiful islands.

"You believe we've fallen from grace, but people are worshipping us in different ways. They come to visit the temples and ruins associated with ancient Greece. They buy our images. We inspire a kind of nostalgia for a simpler time amongst modern people."

From the narrow streets of tourist shops, they emerged into Monastiraki. Stalls of fresh fruit lined the walls outside the metro station. The Disney characters continued to dance in front of tourist children, hoping to persuade eager youngsters to beg for photographs.

"Ten euros for a selfie!" demanded Mickey Mouse.

"Oh, please, Dad," pleaded a seven-year-old daughter.

"This is Athens, darling, not Euro Disney! Mickey's on holiday. He doesn't live here!"

"Pleeese, Mom," begged the daughter, with tears starting to well in her eyes.

Artemis eyed Mickey with an air of disgust. "That definitely makes the case for divine intervention!" she muttered.

The gods tested ice cream cones while sitting on a low wall, watching the activity in the square.

Eventually, Athena suggested, "There's a cocktail bar six floors up at the side of the square. There are beautiful views of the Acropolis from up there. If we head up before it starts to get dark, we can watch the sun go down and the Parthenon light up."

"That sounds good to me," said Persephone approvingly. "Cocktail sundowners and a party worthy of the gods."

Chapter 15: The Cocktail Bar

On the rooftop lounge of the Athena Cocktail Bar, the three teachers relaxed at an edge table with an unobstructed view across Monastiraki and the Agora ruins to the Acropolis. The sun was disappearing behind the horizon to the west, and the illuminations were now highlighting the ancient buildings, rock faces and supporting walls below, turning the white rocks and building materials various shades of orange. Resembling a huge layer cake, the Acropolis, upon which the Parthenon formed the candle-lit top layer, dominated central Athens.

"Isn't that just gorgeous, ladies?" said Daphne. "We need to get some pics."

A few minutes earlier, they had ordered drinks at the bar. The barman, sporting a name badge labelled 'Achilles', was tall, attractive, slim, and slightly muscular. He had brown, suggestive eyes and white teeth that smiled from ear to ear. With a Greek tan under an open white shirt, wearing tight trousers and polished shoes, he easily caught the three pairs of eyes.

"Ooh, he's lovely," whispered Chloe to Tara.

"Looks like a player if you ask me," replied Tara.

"What can I make for you ladies? One of my special cocktails? Sex on the Beach, maybe?"

"Told you so," Tara said back to Chloe.

"We'll just start with a litre jug of sangria, please," replied Daphne.

"Nothing more exciting?" asked Achilles.

"Maybe later," said Chloe, with a wink. "The night is still a bit young to hit the cocktails."

As they sat enjoying the view, Achilles' understudy, Yannis, brought them three glasses and a jug of red liquid rich in chopped fruit. A friendly face but smaller, duller, and less obviously attractive than Achilles, Yannis was, nevertheless, pleasant and seemingly obliging.

Looking at the waiter's name badge, Daphne addressed him with a friendly smile, "Hey, Yannis, thank you for bringing our drinks."

"Don't mention it, lovely lady. That's what I'm here for. Is there anything else I can do for you?" he added, placing a dish of roasted peanuts on the table.

"Well, actually, would you mind taking some photos for us?"

"Of course. Of course. Very happy to," Yannis responded.

Chloe selected the camera app on her mobile phone and then passed it to Yannis. He proceeded to take several pictures of the three girls, clinking glasses of sangria, then posing with the Monastiraki Square in the foreground beneath them and the Acropolis as a dramatic backdrop. Having thanked Yannis for taking the pictures, they settled in their seats, chatting and sipping their drinks while looking out over the busy scene below.

There were about twenty tables in the rooftop bar. About two-thirds of them were occupied, but the teachers had arrived reasonably early in the evening, so they had managed to grab a prime position overlooking the square, ideal for their posed pictures. While they were soaking up the romantic scene before them, a group of three tables close by became available when their occupants left. Just at that moment, another group of customers arrived and moved towards the free tables.

"Oh no, guess who's here?" said Chloe, looking at the approaching group.

"Good evening, ladies." Hermes greeted them with a friendly smile as he sat at the immediately adjacent table, where he was quickly joined by Hephaestus and Dionysus.

"Hello," Daphne answered. "We keep bumping into each other."

"Are we destined to meet? I'm Hermes, this is Hephaestus, and that is Dionysus."

"Oh, I see. You're doing some sort of Greek gods convention, or are you actors or something?" replied Daphne.

"No, we're the real deal. We're Greek gods," beamed Hermes.

"Hermes! Now you've given away our secret!" snapped Hephaestus.

The three teachers looked at each other and laughed gently at Hermes.

"Not just actors. Clowns, too!" added Chloe.

"Careful what you say, young lady. Hera will get very angry if you insult us gods!" said Hermes.

"Hera? Which one is she?" asked Tara.

"The very elegant lady in the purple dress with the peacock motif."

"Ah, yes. I think she may already be angry with me, but I don't know why," Tara added. "She glared at me when we were up on Areopagus Hill and again at the pavement bar."

"It's really Zeus that she's angry with, but she takes out her anger on the targets of his lust," Hermes explained.

"You're obviously very good actors, and I can see that you really want to get into character. But don't you think it's going a bit too far to frighten innocent passersby?" asked Daphne.

Hera was sitting with Zeus, Athena and Ares at the furthest away of their three tables. Artemis, Persephone, Apollo and Aphrodite sat in between, providing a buffer between her and the three teachers. Luckily, Hera was facing away from the girls, paying more attention to where Zeus was looking.

"I don't think we frighten people," said Hephaestus. "With you, ladies, we'll be on our best behaviour, and we'll keep Hera away from you."

"Thank you, Hephaestus," said Tara, deciding it was best to go along with the god game.

"If you're Greek gods, why aren't you dressed in costume?" asked Chloe. "Apart from Athena and Hera in the ancient Greek-style dresses, you're all wearing bohemian stuff, like a bunch of smart but casual hippies."

"We like to blend with the people. You wouldn't take us seriously if we dressed like three-thousand-year-old warriors," replied Hephaestus.

"So, tell me, what drink would Dionysus recommend?" Tara enquired.

Patting the gourd that hung from his shoulder, Dionysus responded, "This is my own special brew, but they don't sell it here. You ladies should probably stick to the Athena Bar cocktails."

The ladies enjoyed the chat with the gods, playing the game but not taking it seriously. As the conversation continued, topics shifted to focus more on their experiences around Athens, their opinions on tourism and how much they loved the city. However, they also described to Hermes how they had an encounter with a pair of eagles in the region near Mount Olympus.

"That must have been terrifying for you," said Hermes.

"Not at all," replied Daphne. "It was fascinating. I loved seeing those eagles so close."

"Maybe it was Zeus and Hera, disguised as eagles?" suggested Hermes.

"Oh, Hermes, you're such a comedian," laughed Chloe.

As the group chatted, Yannis returned to the tables, carrying cocktails that the gods had ordered.

"Not drinking Dionysus's elixir then?" asked Tara.

"That's for later," replied Dionysus. "We'll test the local cocktails first."

"What have you ordered, then?" Chloe enquired.

"Mine's a Mai-Tai, Dionysus is on Caribbean Punch, and Hephaestus is having the Hot Aphrodite," Hermes replied.

"Hot Aphrodite? That sounds interesting." Daphne suggested.

"I don't actually like it, but the idea of consuming a Hot Aphrodite is appealing. It's as close as I get!" remarked Hephaestus.

The group laughed with Hephaestus, sympathetic to his marital situation but amused by his nonchalance.

"What's in it?" Asked Chloe.

"Ouzo, chocolate-mint liqueur, crème de menthe and fresh cream."

"Oh, that sounds lovely," said Tara. "I think I'll have one of those."

"You ladies would like more drinks?" asked Yannis, noting that the sangria jug was now empty.

"Yes, please. Can I have a Mojito?" asked Daphne.

"I'll have a Piña Colada," added Chloe.

"And a Hot Aphrodite for me," said Tara.

"Another Hot Aphrodite," Yannis said loudly, beaming suggestively as he took the order.

Hera had been aware of the ongoing conversation and laughter between the teachers and the three minstrels. However, until that moment, she had chosen to take no notice. It was best that she kept her eye on Zeus, making sure he did not get involved. But when Yannis exclaimed, "Another Hot

Aphrodite!" to the amusement of the teachers, Hera's face turned a darker purple than her dress. These girls had attracted the attention of her husband and were now mocking the goddess of love!

For the next hour or two, Hera fumed in anger but did her best to stay engaged in conversation with Zeus, Athena and Ares. Cocktails were consumed, conversation was had, jokes were told, and laughter prevailed throughout the rooftop bar. The teachers' conversation occasionally also included Apollo, Artemis, Persephone and Aphrodite, who were in the middle 'buffer' table.

Aphrodite did not take offence at anybody testing the 'Hot Aphrodite'. As usual, she loved the attention it always brought her. She was more distracted by wondering how she and Ares might be able to sneak away from the other gods.

As the evening progressed, Ares was heard to comment on the content of the cocktails on more than one occasion.

"They're giving short measures here!" he complained. "It's all ice and water, with a bit of fruit juice. Those three girls would have fallen off their chairs by now if those cocktails had been properly mixed!"

The teachers were all considerably tipsy, but none as drunk as they should have been, given the amount of alcohol they believed they'd consumed. The effect of the drinks was more on their bladders than on their state of alertness at that point of the evening.

Tara rose from the table, excusing herself as she headed towards the ladies' room. Her movements didn't go unnoticed by the queen of the gods, who decided this might be a moment to strike the fear of a goddess into one of the apparent objects of her husband's roving eye. Two or three minutes after Tara had left the table, Hera also rose and walked towards the ladies' toilets.

As Tara washed her hands, Hera entered the ladies' and stepped towards her. Hera turned to look the teacher in the eye, glaring angrily.

"I should have scratched your eyes out on the beach," she growled.

"What beach? What have I done?" she spluttered in horror.

"You attracted my husband. You showed him your naked body and fed him cheese," snapped Hera.

This woman's crazy, thought Tara. *I'll just steer clear.* "You must be mistaking me for somebody else," Tara responded, trying her best to smile as she quickly exited the ladies' washroom before Hera could say any more.

Returning to the table in a state of shock, she sat down quietly.

"You look pale, Tara. Are you OK?" asked Daphne.

"I've just been attacked by Hera!"

"Attacked? Did she touch you?"

"No. She just threatened to scratch my eyes out!"

"She's just taking their god game too seriously. Pretending she's a very angry, jealous queen of the gods with an unfaithful husband," said Chloe.

"But there's more," added Tara. "She said I'd shown her husband my naked body and fed him cheese! Maybe they really are the eagles! How else could she know that?"

"You told Hermes and co about our experience with the eagles. Maybe she overheard, or somebody told her?" suggested Chloe.

Having noticed Tara's anxiety and heard the girls talking since she returned from the toilets, Hermes leaned towards the teacher's table once more. "I couldn't help overhearing what you were saying. Are you OK?" he asked Tara.

"Just a bit worried. I think Hera is taking this god game a bit too seriously," Tara replied.

"You'd be best to just keep your distance from her. She really does believe that she's the queen of the gods."

"I thought there was something wrong with her earlier; now I know. She's delusional. If any of us have to interact with her, we'd better just make sure we talk and curtsey as if she really is a queen," Tara suggested.

Despite the unwanted malice from Hera and the apparent shortage of alcohol in their cocktails, the three teachers were determined to enjoy their last night in Athens to the fullest. They were enjoying the conversation with the rest of the gods, even when that meant playing along with the 'god game'.

The backdrop was a romantic vista of ancient Athens and the Acropolis. Bouzouki music floated in from neighbouring bars. The smell of street food, herbs and spices overpowered any odours from blocked sewers. The constant murmur of people chatting and laughing in the streets below exuded warmth and happiness. It was a friendly place where everybody was partying and having fun.

As midnight rolled by, the other customers had gradually left the rooftop bar. Yannis, too, bade his farewell as he went off duty, leaving the bar in the hands of his manager, Achilles.

Achilles now took on the role of waiter as well as cocktail mixer. He placed a glass of Hot Aphrodite, which was now Ares' favourite, on the table by the god of war. Ares lifted the glass, examined the contents and took a sip. Before Achilles could escape the table, Ares had caught his eye.

"Wait, barman!" the war god commanded.

"Do you have a problem, sir?" asked Achilles.

"What is this drink?"

"Hot Aphrodite as you ordered, sir," replied Achilles, becoming nervous.

"This is supposed to have mint-chocolate liqueur and crème de menthe, but it's mainly mint cordial. And it's full of ice. I can hardly taste the ouzo."

"Maybe the ice bucket slipped when I was filling the glass. Perhaps I can mix you another, sir?"

"Wait!" commanded Ares again.

Picking up in turn each of the cocktails that Achilles had delivered, he examined the drink, then tasted it. After each, he raised his eyebrows in a look of disgust, then glared at Achilles.

"You have done the same with all of these. They're full of water and ice, with very small spirit and liqueur measures!"

"If you prefer, I can remix the full round of drinks, sir," responded Achilles, trying to stop his knees from trembling.

Ares had found an outlet for his anger—a battle he knew he could win. He looked around the assembled gods, then turned again to Achilles.

"Achilles is your name, is it? You are not fit to grovel at the feet of the Achilles who no doubt your parents named you after. No, we don't want you to remix the drinks. I'm going to teach you how to make them instead. My friend Dionysus knows a little about mixing cocktails, so maybe he and Hermes can be my assistants for a little lesson."

Achilles swallowed hard. He knew he was guilty of producing weak cocktails, especially towards the end of the evening. Customers were less likely to notice as they became more drunk. A bit more fruit juice, water and ice, and a bit less of the spirit measures. It meant the customers didn't get drunk so quickly, so they might buy more drinks. It also meant better profits. If he mixed some cocktails for himself, it wouldn't be noticed as there always seemed to be excess stock.

Ares stood up in front of Achilles, who was neither short nor weak in appearance. However, he suddenly felt very small and vulnerable before this giant of a man who was solid muscle, like an ancient warrior, which, of course, he was!

"Come with me, Achilles," ordered Ares, placing a huge hand on one shoulder and steering him towards the bar like a child's toy.

Hermes and Dionysus followed behind, curious to see what Ares would do next. At the bar, the war god ordered the barman to mix a Hot Aphrodite right there on the counter so that they could all see exactly what went into the mixer.

Achilles carefully poured all the ingredients according to a recipe book he kept behind the bar: 25ml ouzo, 25ml crème de menthe, 30ml mint-chocolate liqueur, and 30ml fresh cream. He then shook the mixture and decanted it into a 250ml glass to which he added a sensible amount of ice, some black grapes and a few mint leaves.

Ares took a small sip of the cocktail and smiled approvingly. “That’s very tasty,” he said with an uncharacteristic, friendly smile.

Achilles was relieved.

“Now down it!” commanded Ares, the friendly smile transforming into an aggressive glare.

Achilles had no choice. He enjoyed the cocktail but would have preferred to sip it over half an hour rather than knock it back.

“OK. What’s next?” Ares said. “Hermes, you had a very watery Mai-Tai. I think Achilles needs to learn that one, too. Don’t you think?”

Hermes was not going to disagree with Ares. “If you say so, Ares.”

"A Mai-Tai next, please, barman," came the order. "Bacardi, rum, amaretto, Curaçao, lemon and lime juice. And make sure they're all good measures."

Achilles mixed the drink carefully. Hermes sipped and approved, and then came the order.

"Down it, barman!"

And the process continued. Caribbean Punch, Mojito, Piña Colada, Bloody Mary, Black Russian!

Ares demanded the mixing, approval and drinking of about a dozen cocktails before the barman asked for permission to be sick. The three teachers watched in horror.

"Poor Achilles," said Chloe. He's going to get alcohol poisoning if they push him any further."

"Best you don't get involved," suggested Hephaestus. "You'd just get on the wrong side of Hera again. She might suggest you share the cocktails with Achilles!"

The girls watched on in silent horror, praying that they would stop soon and allow Achilles to empty his intestines. After Achilles had thrown up a few times and was losing the ability to stand upright, Ares steered him once more to the edge tables overlooking the Monastiraki Square.

"Now, my friend Achilles," muttered Ares, "hopefully you know a bit more about how to mix cocktails. But if you need a reminder of what should really happen to people who rip off their customers, then maybe this'll help. I seem to remember the first Achilles had a weak spot. The heel, wasn't it?"

Ares reached down and grabbed Achilles by his left heel. The war god lifted him up suddenly, stepping forward. The barman found himself upside-down, hanging outside the parapet of the rooftop bar. From the sixth floor, the pavement looked a long way down.

One or two people in the street below thought they were witnessing a skirmish but were dazzled by the rooftop lighting. The teachers began to scream.

"Oh no, he's going to kill the barman!" yelled Tara.

Aphrodite decided that, while Ares was obviously trying to teach a lesson to a wrong-doer, he was now going a bit too far.

"Let him go, Ares!" yelled Aphrodite.

Maybe it was appropriate that Ares was clutching Achilles by his heel. He didn't intend to drop the barman but reacted instinctively in response to his lover's call, obediently opening his hand.

All present watched in horror as Achilles began his descent towards the pavement.

It is often intriguing how, in matters of life and death, the passage of time may not flow smoothly. Sometimes, an instant may seem like a lifetime, while at other times, a life may be over in an instant. In the supernatural world, time itself may be allowed to stand still when required.

Zeus and Hera looked at each other as their son's apparent intervention in the life of Achilles began to play out its role. Knowing that it's the Moirai, aka the Fates, rather than the gods, who determine when a man's life should end, they took the only action they could: they visited the Fates.

The Fates are three sisters, Clotho, Lachesis and Atropos, daughters of the Titaness Themis and of Zeus himself. They live in a cave near the end of the Earth, where they have the form of elderly, haggard ladies gathered around a spinning wheel. When a mortal is born, Clotho spins out the thread of his life, Lachesis measures it to an exact length, and Atropos hovers with a pair of scissors ready to cut the thread when it reaches the length measured by Lachesis.

The Moirai curtseyed respectfully as the king and queen of the gods appeared in their cavern.

"Father Zeus," said Clotho, "it is unusual to see you here at the end of the Earth. What service do you require of us?"

Clearing his throat, Zeus began to explain, "Well, it's about Achilles, the bar manager at the Athena Cocktail Bar in

Monastiraki. It's just that he's about to die as a result of action by my son, your half-brother, Ares. Can you tell us if his thread is at the correct length?"

Lachesis held out her measuring tape while examining the thread that Clotho had spun for Achilles.

"No, Father Zeus," confirmed Lachesis. "Achilles still has many years to come."

"Thank you, daughters," Zeus said, exhaling with relief. "It seems further intervention is required. We take your leave."

"Bye, Father," said Clotho.

"Bye, Father," added Lachesis.

"Bye, Father," said Atropos, waving her scissors. "Nice to see you, even for a brief moment."

The three teachers on the roof bar gasped in horror as they saw Achilles' heel slip away from Ares' grasp. Then, as he began to accelerate downward, a deafening boom reverberated around the roof, accompanied by a blinding flash of light. A huge lightning strike on a clear, early summer evening?

Although Daphne, Chloe and Tara were blinded by the light, they were all sure they had seen the silhouettes of two huge eagles diving down the side of the building. Ears buzzing after the thunderclap, they rubbed their eyes while they recovered from the dazzling light. As their vision cleared, they all witnessed a terrified Achilles sitting on the floor in front of the bar.

"What just happened?" asked Chloe. "Did you see two eagles?"

"I think we were struck by lightning," replied Tara. "Yes, I saw the eagles. How did the barman get back there?"

"Either he bounced back up somehow, or the eagles rescued him!" exclaimed Daphne.

"It was the eagles," said Chloe. "I saw them drop him on the floor."

Aware that no mortals should be allowed to witness divine intervention, Hermes decided that action must be taken to confuse the witnesses.

"Dionysus, these ladies need something to calm their nerves after what they've just seen."

Nodding in agreement, Dionysus poured a good measure of his elixir from the gourd he always carried into the ladies' empty cocktail glasses.

"Drink this, ladies. It'll make you feel better," Hermes asserted.

"How do we know this isn't spiked?" asked Tara with concern.

"Trust me," replied Hermes, smiling in reassurance.

The teachers obediently sipped the contents of the glasses until they were empty. Apollo approached each of them in turn.

"Your eyes look glazed, Daphne. Do you feel OK?"

"Yea, whaa, shhuresh," she slurred.

"Look into my eyes, Daphne," Apollo instructed her in a commanding voice. "Tomorrow, you will remember having an enjoyable party in the cocktail bar. You may remember some blurred details, but dreams and reality will be mixed. You will blame your memory loss on the strength of the cocktails."

"Yesshh, shirrr," she slurred, drooling slightly.

Apollo repeated his hypnosis with each of the teachers and then applied the same process to Achilles.

In the street below, a number of people had been staring up at the rooftop bar. Confused stories were circulating among them. The building had been struck by lightning. Some people thought a man had been held over the edge of the roof and possibly even fallen, but there was no body, no blood. Other rumours of two huge birds were whispered among the group.

"Probably seen by somebody who'd drunk too much," asserted some of the crowd.

"So, can we carry on partying now?" asked Persephone.

"I think it would be sensible to clear up here and get these ladies back to their hotel room," said Zeus.

Hera glared at him accusingly. "*I'll* take charge of taking the teachers to their rooms. Artemis, Persephone and Athena will help me."

"Where are Aphrodite and Ares?" asked Persephone.

"Probably in a toilet cubicle somewhere," responded Hephaestus indifferently.

After restoring the room to a reasonable state, the gods agreed it was time to take their leave and return to their various bases.

"I'll come back to Athens soon, Athena," Persephone assured her. "We can laugh at the world together."

"That'll be fun, Perse," she replied, "and I'll come and join you on that beach in Naxos sometime soon, too."

"Hey, don't forget me, girls," added Artemis. "Always happy to join you for a good chinwag."

Reluctantly, Athena had to accept that, even though Zeus had decreed divine intervention was permitted, in reality, that could not lead to a new era of significance for the Olympians. As fictitious, imaginary characters, nothing they could do would change the truth of human progress and its consequences. But strangely, it didn't really seem to matter anymore. In the mythological world, she had enjoyed the reunion and rekindled friendships with the other gods, particularly with Persephone, who would be a new soul mate in the future. Well, at least for six months of the year. From now on, she would enjoy watching mortal life roll by with good grace.

Chapter 16: Postscript

Achilles awoke from what had seemed to be a horrible dream. Looking up, he realised he was still in the cocktail bar. "I must have slept on the floor," he pondered.

His head hurt like Zeus's had done when Hephaestus had split it with an axe to release Athena. His mouth felt like something horrible had died in it. His stomach kept threatening to spray the walls. Vague memories crept back to him: people pretending to be Greek gods, teaching him how to mix cocktails; the horror of looking down the wall of the tower block to the pavement below, waiting to be dropped, falling and being grabbed by huge birds in the middle of a lightning strike!

"Did I dream all that?" he asked himself.

Scanning the cocktail bar, he could see that the tables had all been cleared. The bottles behind the bar were all reasonably full, like on any other morning. The cocktail bar had been cleaned while he slept. He checked the till. There were good takings from the previous night.

It's all too normal, he thought. *Must have been a dream. Maybe I should drink less cocktails.*

So divine intervention played its role in making sure Achilles carried on serving cocktails. He hadn't died for adding too much water and ice, at least, not on this occasion. However, he felt a strange conscience telling him that he would never over-water/over-ice the cocktails in the future. Only good measures of spirits and liqueurs would be used. In fact, he would make the Athena Cocktail Lounge the best bar in Athens. Generous measures at reasonable prices. Happy Hours to die for, but not yet!

On the Acropolis, Athena found herself fretting at the behaviour of tourists, just as before the reunion. Zeus had permitted divine intervention, provided it was only used by imaginary beings. She smiled to herself. She would stalk litter droppers on the rock and give them the evil eye if they didn't pick up their rubbish. And maybe give an occasional bladder squeeze!

On the little island at the end of Nissi Beach, Aphrodite sunned herself. She put up with the occasional comments from irritating yob tourists. If truth be told, she quite enjoyed the attention, knowing that they were usually too much in awe of her beauty to actually approach a stunning lady who was way above their league. Besides, she had acquired a little phial of

Athena's potion, which could prove useful if needed. Additionally, she would have more frequent visits from Ares, who had given up on trying to influence the Ukraine War and shifted his focus to Palestine, which was much more convenient for visiting Cyprus.

After 10,000 years of being cuckolded, Hephaestus considered it best to take no notice of Aphrodite's activities with the war god. Partying, busking, and playing cards on the beaches and bars of the Greek Islands would be sufficient for most people, even immortals. Besides, the companionship of Hermes, Dionysus and Apollo formed an amiable brotherhood. Had they chosen to become a rock band, they would have been bigger and lasted much longer than even The Rolling Stones.

Persephone had enjoyed her visit to Athens and agreed with Athena that they should meet much more regularly. She was happy at the taverna in Naxos, with Hestia, Demeter and Dionysus for company, but had found that she and Athena enjoyed watching the world go by together, and a regular get-together would be good for both of them. They had found an excellent cocktail bar with a stunning view of the Acropolis and perfect cocktails. That could become their regular venue.

Zeus soared high above the Aegean beaches, stretching his wings but looking over his shoulder more often than searching the ground below. And she was always there! A little above and behind him: Hera! Ready to dive on him if he chose to glide away from the straight and narrow flight path.

Bernard and Justin enjoyed the rest of their short holiday in Mykonos, sunning themselves, drinking and dancing. Bernard flirted with several gay guys, and both of them were generally having a good time. However, nobody else that they met had the enigmatic charisma of the twins from Delos and the minstrels they met on the beach.

Apollo was the most beautiful man Bernard had ever seen. Hermes was charming, cheeky and a bit devious. Hephaestus was obviously clever, but too straight to be of interest to Bernard. Dionysus had looked a bit evil, but that was mainly due to his hungover eyes, which was hardly surprising, given the rocket fuel he was drinking.

Justin already knew that Bernard's behaviour would be camp and flirtatious, so he was not the least surprised at how he had swooned in the presence of Apollo and bantered with Hermes. In Justin's opinion, Artemis was the best of the bunch. Gorgeous, but intelligent and somehow asexual. He could imagine her as a close platonic friend, with no need for anything other than philosophical interaction.

They had all been wonderful actors, so convincing as Greek gods. The musicians had been out of this world, and the music was so hypnotic. It was a pity they hadn't had any CD copies with them and didn't mention whether they had anything on YouTube or a website.

And as for that fire water, absinthe, nectar or whatever they wanted to call it, it was something that blew away the tastebuds. Sadly, they didn't even know what it was really called or which shelf to find it on in the supermarket.

Mykonos had been fun, but the gods had made the trip magical. Meeting them had turned the trip into an experience that would never be forgotten by both Bernard and Justin. Without that interaction, Mykonos would have simply been an overpriced tourist-ridden holiday resort.

The three teachers nursed sore heads the morning after the night before. Everything seemed to be a blur. They could remember going to the cocktail bar but had only vague, dreamy recollections of what had happened there. There had been a strange group of people. Daphne held an image of one character, a bearded man who kept looking at her and then turning into an eagle. Then there was his wife, who kept kicking him before diving at him with open talons, ready to tear eyes out.

She was sure it had all been a strange dream, somehow mixing with events from the beach near Mount Olympus.

"Did somebody get thrown off the roof last night?" asked Chloe.

"Yes, I remember that!" exclaimed Tara before adding, "Or maybe they just threatened to do it?"

"You both remember them too?" said Daphne. "Those strange people pretending to be Greek gods."

"Did we just imagine all that?" asked Chloe.

"No, Chloe, we all remember something. Strange people, threatening to kill the barman," added Daphne. "And then there was that lightning strike. Lucky it didn't kill us all!"

"It's been a great holiday, girls," said Tara, "but nobody will believe any of our stories. They'll just think we were permanently pissed!"

"Just think about it," said Daphne, "us feeding a golden eagle bits of cheese on the beach, then another one attacking it and stealing my camera!"

"And then those strange people pretending to be Greek gods and threatening to kill the barman!" added Tara.

"Well, Daph, you've still got the video footage of the eagles. We can tell the story, place bets with anybody who doesn't believe us, and then show them the footage as proof."

"Tits 'n' all," giggled Chloe.

The three laughed raucously, then clutched their splitting heads. They took some painkillers and packed their bags.

"OK, girls," said Chloe. "Our flight back to Liverpool is in three hours' time. The taxi should be waiting."

With that, they headed off on their journey home after a trip to Athens that would remain fuzzy but exciting in their memories for a long time to come.

Hector and Helen Johnson sat on canvas sunchairs on the swimming pool deck of their cruise ship. Today, they had a day at sea. After Mykonos, they had a very disappointing visit to Santorini. Lots of time was wasted queuing among crowds to get up to Thira, the iconic image capital of the island. Whitewashed cuboid buildings and blue-painted domes above dark red, igneous cliffs overlooked the still-smoking caldera of the volcano in the sea below, which had blown Santorini apart more than 3000 years ago.

Hundreds of people pushed and elbowed to find a position from which to take the obligatory selfies. Helen had taken numerous shots on her phone, none of them satisfactory.

"Jeez-us!" Hector exclaimed as Helen struggled among the mobs trying to take pictures. "This is like someone filled the Grand Canyon with water!"

"Lucky they can't sail cruise ships up the Grand Canyon, or you'd get the crowds like this all tryin' to get them selfies!" Helen had added.

Eventually, they returned to the ship without spending any money in the overcrowded tourist shops, bars and restaurants.

At sea, it was relatively peaceful, except for the crowds in front of the bar on the pool deck. Slow service seemed to be another obligatory part of the cruise, probably in order to slow down the cocktail consumption of the people who had all-inclusive drinks packages.

Hector thought back to his experience on the Athenian Acropolis. He hadn't peed himself since.

"That damn woman," he reminded himself. "Ah wonder who she was?"

"Did ya say somethin', Hector?" asked Helen.

"Nah, Helen. Just wondrin' what in heaven persuaded us to go on this goddamn boat!"

Hector stared westwards into the future as the Euthanasia Cruises ship, River Styx, carried on sailing slowly towards the setting sun, but that's another story!

Bibliography

The main characters in *Divine Intervention* are the gods of Greek mythology. While most people will be familiar with the names Zeus and Aphrodite, the other gods may be less well-known to many. I have tried to base the characters on their personalities as I have perceived them from descriptions in other works.

I didn't want to repeat the tales from Greek mythology beyond the brief references that help develop the characters within the context of this novel. However, if you have found that my story has stimulated your curiosity, there are many sources available should you wish to read further. For a light and amusing modern take on Greek mythology, I recommend the works of Stephen Fry: *Mythos*, *Heroes* and *Troy*.

A more traditional approach is provided in *The Greek Myths* by Robin and Kathryn Waterfield, or in *Mythology: Timeless Tales of Gods and Heroes* by Edith Hamilton.

The Complete World of Greek Mythology, by Richard Buxton, provides an interesting background to the origin and development of the Greek myths.

The relevant works by the above authors are included below:

Buxton, R. (2004). The Complete World of Greek Mythology.

Fry, Stephen. (2018). Mythos.

Fry, Stephen. (2019). Heroes.

Fry Stephen. (2020). Troy.

Hamilton, Edith. (1942). Mythology: Timeless Tales of Gods and Heroes. (2017 edition).

Waterfield, Robin and Waterfield, Kathryn. (2013). The Greek Myths.

Other Work by Norman George

If you enjoyed reading *Divine Intervention*, then why not take a look at Who Writes the Rules?

ISBN 978-1739233006

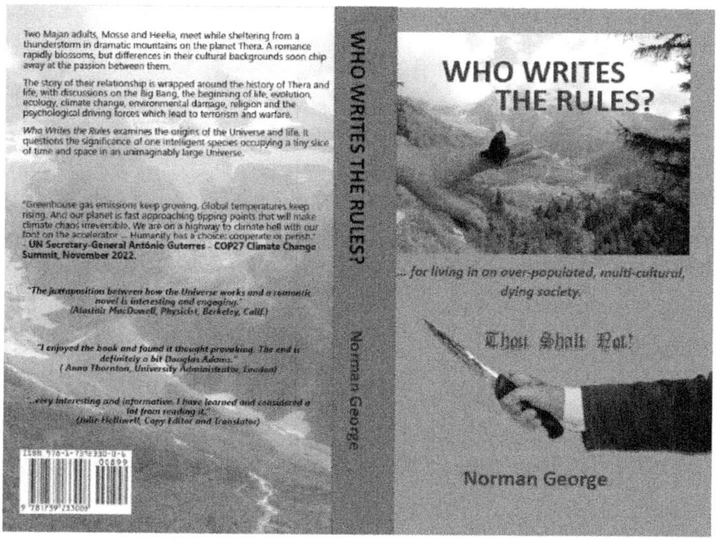

Life in an Alpine resort, in conjunction with his interest in sciences, inspired Norman to write his first novel, *Who Writes the Rules?* He wanted to write about scientific topics that impacted human societies, but he considered that, not being a professional scientist, he would not have sufficient credibility to do this. Therefore, he chose to use a romantic novel, telling the story of a relationship between two people from different cultures, as a vehicle for including scientific discussions. Norman's intention was to persuade readers who wouldn't normally pick up a science book to read discussions on the origins of the Universe and life, evolution, ecology and climate change. The novel combines a serious human story about the two protagonists with enlightening and thought-provoking discussions about topics affecting all of humanity.

Back Cover Text

Two Majan adults, Mosse and Heelia, meet while sheltering from a thunderstorm in dramatic mountains on the planet Thera. A romance rapidly blossoms, but differences in their cultural backgrounds soon chip away at the passion between them.

The story of their relationship is wrapped around the history of Thera and life, with discussions on the Big Bang, the beginning of life, evolution, ecology, climate change, environmental damage, religion and the psychological driving forces which lead to terrorism and warfare.

Who Writes the Rules examines the origins of the Universe and life. It questions the significance of one intelligent species occupying a tiny slice of time and space in an unimaginably large Universe.

"The juxtaposition between how the Universe works and a romantic novel is interesting and engaging."
(Alastair MacDowell, Physicist, Berkeley, Calif.)

"I enjoyed the book and found it thought-provoking. The end is definitely a bit Douglas Adams."
(Anna Thornton, University Administrator, London)

"…very interesting and informative. I have learned and considered a lot from reading it."
(Julie Helliwell, Copy Editor and Translator)

Printed in Great Britain
by Amazon

51974111R00162